LADIES' MAN AT WORK . . .

I spoke up. "If an innocent man is convicted of murdering your sister, the trouble is that the guilty man goes free. Do you want that?"

Stella Fleming focused up at me. Up, because she wasn't more than an inch over five feet. "It's none of your business what I want," she said, and meant it.

"No," I said, "but it's *your* business. I'm not a newshound trying to get a headline, I'm a private detective trying to dig up some facts. I already have some. I know why you won't see reporters, why you have no information for anybody. Because your sister was a doxy, and you—"

"My sister was a what?"

"D,O,X,Y, doxy. I happen to like that better than concubine or paramour or mistress. I don't—"

I stopped because I had to, to protect my face. When a woman flies at you to claw, what you do depends on the woman. If she has real tiger in her you may even have to plug her, but with Stella Fleming, with her short reach, all I had to do was stiff-arm her. . . .

A NERO WOLFE MYSTERY
DEATH OF A DOXY
REX STOUT

BANTAM BOOKS
NEW YORK • TORONTO • LONDON • SYDNEY • AUCKLAND

DEATH OF A DOXY
*A Bantam Book / published by arrangement with
Viking Penguin*

PRINTING HISTORY
Viking edition published August 1966
*Literary Guild One Dollar Book Club edition
published October 1966*
Condensation published in ARGOSY *April 1966 and in*
TORONTO STAR WEEKLY *October 1966*
Bantam edition / August 1967

ISBN 0-553-27606-9

Published simultaneously in the United States and Canada

*Bantam Books are published by Bantam Books, a division of Bantam
Doubleday Dell Publishing Group, Inc. Its trademark, consisting of the
words "Bantam Books" and the portrayal of a rooster, is Registered in U.S.
Patent and Trademark Office and in other countries. Marca Registrada.
Bantam Books, 666 Fifth Avenue, New York, New York 10103.*

PRINTED IN THE UNITED STATES OF AMERICA

RAD   20   19   18   17   16   15   14   13   12   11

I stood and sent my eyes around. It's just routine, when leaving a place where you aren't supposed to be, to consider if and where you have touched things, but that time it went beyond mere routine. I made certain. There were plenty of things in the room—fancy chairs, a marble fireplace without a fire, a de luxe television console, a coffee table in front of a big couch with a collection of magazines, and so forth. Deciding I had touched nothing, I turned and stepped back into the bedroom. Nearly everything there was too soft to take a fingerprint—the wall-to-wall carpet, the pink coverlet on the king-size bed, the upholstered chairs, the pink satin fronts on the three pieces of furniture. I crossed for another look at the body of a woman on the floor a couple of feet from the bed, on its back with the legs spread out and one arm bent. I hadn't had to touch it to check that it was just a body or to see the big dent in the skull, but was there one chance in a million that I had put fingers on the heavy marble ashtray lying there? The butts and ashes that had been in it were scattered around, and it was a good bet that it had made the dent in the skull. I shook my head; I couldn't possibly have been such an ape.

I left. Of course I had to use my handkerchief on the doorknob, inside and outside, and I used a knuckle on the button that summoned the do-it-yourself elevator, and also, in the elevator, on the 1 button. I dabbed the 4 button, which I had pushed coming in, with my handkerchief. There was no one in the little lobby down below, and since I had been gloved when I entered I didn't have to bother about the knobs of the outside door. As I headed west, toward Lexington Avenue, I turned up my overcoat collar and put my gloves on. It was the coldest day of the winter, with a gusty wind.

I don't try to do any hard thinking while I'm walking, you bump into people, but anyway it didn't even call for guessing, let alone thinking. What was needed was asking, and the person to ask lived on the second floor of a walkup on 52nd Street between Eighth and Ninth Avenues. Since this was 39th Street, thirteen short blocks up and four long blocks crosstown. My watch said 4:36. Getting a taxi at that time of day is a career, and there was no hurry. He was on a job. I walked.

It was one minute to five when I entered a phone booth in a bar and grill on Eighth Avenue and dialed a number. When Fritz answered I asked him to buzz the plant rooms, and after a wait a growl came: "Yes?"

"Me," I said. "I've run into a snag on this personal errand and I don't know when I'll be back. Probably not in time for dinner."

"Are you in trouble?"

"No."

"Can I reach you if a need arises?"

"No."

"Very well." He hung up.

He was being tolerant because I was on a personal errand, none of his business. He hates to be bothered when he's up with the orchids, and if the errand had been for him he would have said I should have told Fritz.

Outside again, half a block west, cold-faced but with the blood going good, I entered a vestibule and pushed the button marked Cather. After two more pushes there was still no click—as expected. It was too damn cold to hang around, so I headed back for Eighth Avenue, with a notion about five or six fingers of bourbon, but with me the time for bourbon is when

I'm going to let down, not when I have to pick up, so I went to a drugstore counter instead and got coffee.

When the coffee was down I went to the booth and dialed a number, hung up after ten rings with no answer, returned to the counter, and bought a glass of milk. Another trip to the booth; still no answer, and I ordered a corned beef on rye and coffee. There is never any rye bread in the kitchen of the old brownstone on West 35th Street. It was twenty minutes past six, on my fifth try at the phone, after the second piece of pumpkin pie and the fourth cup of coffee, when a voice said hello.

"Orrie? Archie. You alone?"

"Sure, I'm always alone. Did you go?"

"Yeah. I—"

"What'd you get?"

"I'd rather show you. Expect me in two minutes."

"What the hell, I'll come—"

"I'm in the neighborhood. Two minutes." I hung up.

I didn't stop to put on my overcoat and gloves. Two minutes of near-zero wind is a good test for your staying power. When I pushed the button in the vestibule the click came quick, and when I entered and started up the stairs Orrie called down from the top, "Hell, I could have come."

Once Nero Wolfe, showing off, said to me, "*Vultus est index animi*," and I said, "That's not Greek," and he said, "A Latin proverb. The face is the index of the mind." It depends on whose face and whose mind. Across from you at the poker table, Saul Panzer's face is an index of absolutely nothing. But you keep on trying, and I was still at it on Orrie Cather's face after he showed me in and took my hat and coat and we sat. I sat and eyed him until he demanded, "Can't you place me?"

I said, "*Vultus est index animi.*"

"Good," he said. "I've often wondered. What the hell's eating you?"

"Just curiosity. Is it possible that you're playing me?"

"For God's sake. Playing you how? For what?"

"I wish I knew." I crossed my legs. "Okay, I'll report. I followed the script. I arrived at a quarter past four on the dot, pushed the button several times, got no reaction as expected, used the key you gave me, took the elevator to the fourth floor, used the other key, and entered. No one in the living room, and I went to the bedroom. I don't say someone was there, because properly speaking a corpse is not someone. It was on the floor not far from the bed. I had never seen Isabel Kerr or a picture of her, but I suppose it had been her. A pink thing with lace and pink slippers, no stockings. A couple of—"

"You're saying she was dead?"

"Don't interrupt. A couple of inches over five feet, hundred and ten pounds, well-designed oval face, blue eyes, lots of clover-blossom-honey hair, small ears close—"

"By God. *By God.*"

"Her?"

"Yes."

"Stop interrupting. Mr. Wolfe never does. I didn't have to touch her to check. I mean *it*. There was a bruise on the forehead and a big dent in the skull, two inches above and back of the left ear. On the floor, three feet from her right shoulder, was a marble ashtray which looked heavy enough to dent a thicker skull than hers probably was. There were purple spots on an arm and a leg. Cadaveric lividities to you. Her forehead was good and cold, and—"

"You said you didn't touch her."

"I touch with my fingers. I don't call applying a wrist to a forehead or a leg touching. The leg was cold too. It had been a corpse for at least five hours and probably more. The ashtray had been wiped. There were butts and ashes on the carpet but no particles on the tray. I was in there a total of about six minutes. The idea of staying to look for things didn't appeal to me." I put a hand in a pocket and got something. "Here are your keys."

He didn't see them. His jaw was clamped. He unclamped it to say, "Playing you. For God's sake. Playing you."

"Naturally I'm curious."

He got up and went through a doorway. I tossed the keys onto a table by a window and looked around. It was a good-sized room with three windows, with furniture that would do all right for a bachelor who wasn't fussy. The only light was from a pair of bulbs in a wall bracket, but there was a lamp by an easy chair that wasn't turned on. Orrie came back with a bottle and two glasses and offered me one, but I said no thanks, I had just dined. He put one glass down and poured in the other, took a healthy gulp, made a face, and sat down.

"Playing you," he said. "Nuts. Now you ask me where I've been since eight o'clock this morning and can I prove it."

I shook my head. "Since I'm merely curious, that would be stretching it. If I wanted to be nasty I would have opened up by barking at you something like, 'Why did you leave the ashtray on the floor?' Of course we do have to consider facts, such as the fact that I may be the only one besides you who knows that her being dead pulls a thorn for you. A bad thorn in deep. So of course I'm curious about one detail. Did you kill her?"

"No. My God, Archie. Am I a sap?"

"No. You're no mental giant, but you're not a sap. It would be nice if you could sell me. After all, you pulled me in, you knew I was going there today. It would be extra nice if you were covered."

"I'm not covered." He was staring at me but possibly not seeing me. He took a mouthful of whisky and swallowed it twice. "As I told you, I'm on a job for Bascom. I was out at eight and picked up a subject a little before nine and was on him all day. It was—"

"Single tail?"

"Yes. Just routine. From nine-nineteen until twelve-thirty-five I was in the lobby of an office building."

"No company?"

"No."

"Then I'm still curious. You would be if we traded spots, you know damn well you would, but that's all I am, just curious. Do you want to ask me anything?"

"Yes, I do. You had gloves and keys, I don't mean mine. You knew there might be something there. Why didn't you take a quick look?"

I grinned at him. "You don't mean that."

"The hell I don't."

I nodded. "Now and then you *are* a sap." I stood up. "As you know, Orrie, and as I know, you think it would be fine if you had my job. That's all right, there's nothing wrong with ambition. But what if you had got *too* ambitious? What if you knew there was nothing there to point to you? What if you had arranged for one man, me, to go there at a quarter past four, and for another man, maybe a cop on an anonymous tip, to arrive a few minutes later? It wouldn't have hooked me for murder, since the ME would set the time, but I would have the keys on me, not only yours, and the rubber gloves, and that would have been good for at least a couple of years. Of course I didn't really believe it, but being the nervous type—"

"Balls." He was staying put, his head tilted back. "What are you going to do?"

I looked at my wrist. "Dinner will be half over, and anyway I ate. I'm going home and eat two helpings of *crème Génoise*. You crush eight homemade macaroons and soak them in half a cup of brandy. Put two cups of rich milk, half a cup of sugar, and the finely cut rind of a small orange into—"

"So clown it!" he yelled. "Are you going to tell Wolfe?"

"I'd rather not."

"Are you?"

"As it stands now, no."

"Or Saul or Fred?"

"No. Nor Cramer nor J. Edgar Hoover." I went to the couch for my hat and coat. "Don't do anything you wouldn't expect me to do. You know what doctors call professional courtesy?"

"Yeah."

"I sincerely hope you won't need any."

I went.

2

The New York Times knows how to put things. "It
does not appear that Miss Kerr was employed anywhere or engaged in any regular activity." You can't
beat that, leaving it wide open for all types of minds.

At the little table in the kitchen where I eat breakfast, with the *Times* on the rack facing me, I poured
Puerto Rico molasses on a buckwheat cake and told
Fritz, "It would be a good murder to work on. Walking distance."

At the big table inspecting dried mushrooms, with
an eye on me to know when to start the next cake,
he shook his head and said, "No murder is good to
work on. When it's a murder the doorbell scares me
and I never know if you'll come back alive."

I told him he was just blowing, I had yet to see
him scared, forked a bite of cake and molasses, and
Creole sausage, and started the *Times* piece again. I
knew a lot more than it did, which suited me fine.
The only items that were news to me were that the
body had been discovered by Isabel Kerr's sister Stella, that Stella was the wife of Barry Fleming, who
taught mathematics at the Henry Hudson High School,
that Stella had gone to the apartment a little before
seven o'clock Saturday evening—less than three hours
after I left—that tentatively Isabel had died between
eight o'clock and noon, that Stella wouldn't talk to reporters, and that the police and the District Attorney's
office had begun a thorough investigation. The picture

of Isabel had probably been dug up in the files of a
theatrical agent; she had a chorus-girl smile. The one
of Stella had been snapped as a cop had escorted her
across the sidewalk.

So far, so good. But if the errand I had tackled for
Orrie had been on the level, if he hadn't been playing
me, and I didn't really think he had, there would be
fur flying soon, and when I finished breakfast and
went into the office I turned the radio on. Ten-o'clock
news, nothing. When Wolfe came down from the plant
rooms at eleven o'clock the radio was still on, and
when he had crossed to his desk and settled his bulk
in the only chair that holds it to suit him, he scowled
at the radio and then at me and demanded, "Is there
an urgency?"

"Yes, sir," I said. "Will the Braves play in Milwau-
kee or in Atlanta? Also it's Sunday, the day of rest."

"I thought you had an engagement."

"It's for one o'clock, and I may skip it. The lunch
will be all right, but then a man is going to read
poetry."

"Whose poetry?"

"His."

"Pfui."

"Sure. I think Miss Rowan knew he was hungry
and merely wanted to feed him, but then he said he
would do her and her friends a big favor and she was
stuck. He calls it an epithon because it's an epic and it
takes hours."

A corner of his mouth was up an eighth of an inch.
"Serves you right."

"Yeah. What she did in the car that night was in the
line of duty, but you'll never forgive her. I may not
go."

He flipped a hand. "You will." He went at his copy
of the Sunday *Times*. We get three, a total of twenty
pounds—one for him, one for me, and one for Fritz.

When the noon news still had nothing new about
murder, I decided it would be silly to sit around all
afternoon rassling with the *Times*, holding my breath

for the radio every half-hour, and mounted the two flights to my room. Having already shaved, I had only to change to a clean shirt and one of my four best suits. Downstairs again, I looked in at the kitchen and the office to say I was going. Outside, I headed for the garage on Tenth Avenue where we keep the Heron which Wolfe owns and I drive. On Sundays it is often possible to find a spot to put a car.

At twenty minutes past four I was in a big roomy chair in the living room of Lily Rowan's penthouse on top of a building on 63rd Street, leaning back with my eyes closed, trying to decide which one I would rather have, Willie Mays or Sandy Koufax, on my team. The poet, a long-faced specimen with whiskers, who didn't look hungry, but of course had recently had a good meal, was still going strong, but I had stopped hearing him an hour back. It was just a background noise. At a poke on my shoulder I opened my eyes, and Mimi, the maid, was there. She moved her lips to say "Telephone" without saying it. I pulled myself up and to my feet, went to a door at the corner of the room and on through, crossed to the desk where Lily makes out checks for causes which may be worthy, picked up the phone, and told it, "This is Archie Goodwin."

Wolfe's voice said, "I presume you read about the murder of a woman named Isabel Kerr."

I said yes.

"So did I. Mr. Parker is here. He received a telephone call from Orrie Cather, asking him to come to the police station on Twentieth Street, and he went. Orrie is in custody as a material witness. He gave Mr. Parker some information, not much, and told him to consult you. Why?"

"Because. Parker's still there?"

"Yes."

"I'll be there in twenty minutes."

I hung up, went to the kitchen and told Mimi to tell Lily, went to the foyer for my coat and hat, let myself out, and summoned the elevator. The car was around the corner on Madison Avenue. When I was in it and going, turning to head west, I told my mind it might as well go right on with Willie Mays and Sandy Koufax. There was absolutely nothing else for it to do, and wouldn't be until I had heard Parker. As I turned into the garage I decided definitely for Willie Mays. Koufax's arm was too much of a gamble. So I felt I had accomplished something as I walked to the old brownstone, mounted the stoop, let myself in, ditched my coat and hat, and went to the office.

Nathaniel Parker, the lawyer Wolfe uses when he has to, was in the red leather chair with a bottle of scotch, one of soda, a bowl of ice, and a glass on the stand at his elbow. Wolfe was at his desk, with beer. Since he skips his afternoon session in the plant rooms on Sundays, that is his biggest beer day. I hadn't seen Parker for a couple of months, and he rose to shake hands. I told Wolfe, "This is going to be worse than listening to poetry," went to my desk, whirled my chair around, sat, and told Parker, "If you're going to spring him I'd rather wait till I see him."

"It would be a long wait," Parker said. "I think they'll keep him. The way they look and talk."

"A murder charge?"

"Not yet, but I think it soon will be. Perhaps tomorrow."

Wolfe growled at me, "Did he kill that woman? Was that your personal errand yesterday?"

"Let's keep it cool," I suggested. "If he said to consult me, I have to know exactly how he said it." To Parker: "If you don't mind?"

"Certainly." The lawyer took a sip and put the glass down. "He didn't say much. He had refused to answer any questions, any at all, until he saw me. Of course he knows the rules. But also he wouldn't open up with me. He wouldn't even tell me if he had known the woman or had any connection with her. He told me just three things. One, he hadn't killed her and hadn't been near her or her apartment at any time yesterday. Two, where he *had* been yesterday.

Three, I should see you, and you should decide what to tell me. When I left, it was understood that he would tell them of his whereabouts and movements yesterday and stand mute on everything else, and that I would see him tomorrow, after I had talked with you."

"You're acting for him?"

"I agreed to, yes. Provisionally until I had seen you."

"It's up to me?"

"Yes. He said to tell you that he wants you to decide how to handle it."

"That's just dandy. To be trusted like that, I do appreciate it. Excuse me while I rub my nose." I rubbed it with a fingertip, my eyes focused on the big globe over by the bookshelves but not seeing it. It didn't take long because it was really quite simple; it was all or nothing, and it didn't matter if Parker got it now or tomorrow.

I stood up. "I thought you played bridge on winter Sundays."

"I do. The call from Cather intruded."

"Then I suggest that you go back and resume. I have decided how to handle it. I'm going to report to Mr. Wolfe. I'd rather have him glare at me while I'm telling him than while I'm telling you. I'll tell you later, or he will, say tomorrow morning. If you prefer, you can wait in the front room, but it will take a while."

Wolfe, his lips pressed so tight he didn't have any mouth, reached for a bottle and poured beer. Parker looked at him, picked up his glass and emptied it, put the glass down, rose, looked at me, and said, "You might tell me one thing, to be regarded as a privileged communication, did he kill her?"

"Even granting that I know," I said, "it wouldn't be privileged. I'm not your client."

I headed for the hall, but out by the rack I stood and held his coat for a couple of minutes while he exchanged words with Wolfe. Finally he came, took his time getting his scarf adjusted, his overcoat buttoned, and his gloves on, and pulled his shoulders in as a gust hit him when he crossed the sill. When I re-entered the office Wolfe had opened his current book, *Invitation to an Inquest*, by Walter and Miriam Schneir. That was childish. He was rubbing it in that his Sunday-afternoon reading had been ruined, first by Orrie and now by me. I said as I sat, "If you're in the middle of a chapter there's no rush."

He made a noise, put the book down, and glared.

"Friday afternoon," I said, "day before yesterday, Orrie phoned and asked me to meet him that evening. You may remember that I wasn't here to help with the capon Souvaroff, which I regretted. I met Orrie at seven o'clock at Giordano's, a restaurant on West Thirty-ninth Street. I now—"

"Don't cram it," he snapped.

"I won't. I now report what he told me. He was up a stump. He was going to marry a girl named Jill Hardy, an airline stewardess. He showed me a picture of her. They had set a date early in May, when she would have a vacation coming. But it had hit a snag. Another girl, by name Isabel Kerr, was objecting. She had the idea of marrying Orrie herself, and also the idea that he was, or would be, the father of the baby she expected to have in about seven months. She intended to make an issue of it, in public if necessary. She said she had in her possession, presumably in a locked drawer in her apartment, or possibly stashed somewhere, certain objects she could use. One of the objects was his private investigator's license, which she had lifted from his pocket one night about a month ago. Also some pictures and letters, and perhaps other items that Orrie didn't know about. The big point wasn't that she could hook him, but that she could queer him with Jill Hardy."

Wolfe grunted. "She couldn't force him to marry her. Why marry at all?"

"Sure. That's your slant, but it wasn't Orrie's. He wanted the objects, and he was pretty sure they were in the apartment. He knew she spent two or three afternoons a week at the movies, and nearly always Saturday afternoons. He had keys. The idea was that I was to go there the next day, Saturday, now yesterday, at a quarter past four, ring the bell, get no response, go in and up, and look around. I didn't care for it much. Such a chore for Saul or Fred, of course, but while I have nothing against Orrie, I wouldn't borrow his socks. He pointed out that I wouldn't be out on a limb, no matter what. If she was there and answered the bell I would bow out. Almost certainly she wouldn't come before I left, but if she or anyone did I could just be polite; I hadn't broken and entered, I had used keys which she had given him."

"So you went," Wolfe growled.

"Don't rush me. I told him nothing doing unless I had the whole picture. It took a while and a lot of questions, but I had to know if Isabel Kerr was something hot, like the runaway daughter of an ambassador. No. She had formerly been a showgirl, but three years ago had been rescued and installed in the nest she was still occupying. The toughest detail to get was the name of the rescuer. Orrie claimed he didn't know, but of course he did, and I insisted. His name is Avery Ballou, president of the Federal Holding Corporation. Apparently Isabel had some quality that he enjoyed, for he was still paying the rent and the grocery bill and was paying her visits two or three times a week, evenings. But she knew that kind of setup never lasts forever, and anyway she wanted Orrie. They had met somewhere, that's irrelevant and immaterial, about a year ago, and she had been—well, feeding him some of Avery Ballou's groceries, and she had decided she had to have him for keeps. I accepted that. Women don't fall for Orrie quite as fast and furious as he thinks they do, but he is no baboon, and female eyes do sometimes fasten on him."

"So you went."

"Yes. I am not dodging, but I mention that it seemed advisable. While he is no Saul Panzer, for years he has come in very handy for you—okay, for us.

He has done a lot of pretty good chores and has never skunked as far as we know. So I went, yesterday afternoon, with gloves and an assortment of keys, arriving at exactly four-fifteen. There was no answer to my ring, and I went in and up. It's one of those remodeled four-story houses, self-service elevator, no doorman or hallman, and I wasn't seen. Since you have read the piece in the *Times*, you know what I found. I didn't stay to use the gloves or keys; I don't think Orrie rated that. Anyway, even if I found some objects, granting they were there, it was a cinch they would find his prints, since he had been there for hours only three days ago. So I left."

"Seen?"

"No. I phoned you not to expect me for dinner, and—"

"That was at five o'clock."

Just like him. He never seems to notice but he knows. I nodded. "Yeah. I had walked for nearly half an hour, to Orrie's address, or near it. I waited around until he came, saw him in his apartment and told him, and returned his keys. I asked him if he killed her, and he said no. He was on a tailing job for Bascom all day but can't prove it. For the important time, eight o'clock to noon, he's wide open. He wanted to know why I didn't stay for a look. I poked him a little, not much, and came home and ate two helpings of *crème Génoise*. Of course I knew he would be tagged—if nothing else, his prints. That was the urgency on the radio this morning."

"You should have told me."

"What good would it have done? It would only have spoiled the day for you."

"So you went to hear a man read poetry."

I cocked my head. "Look," I said, "you might as well forget me. You're sore and want a target, but I'm not it. Of course, if you forget Orrie too, there is no target and you can go back to your book."

He looked at the book, picked it up, and put it down again. He picked up his glass, frowned at it because the head was gone, drank it anyway, to the bottom, returned the glass to the tray, and pushed the tray aside. "Orrie," he said. "Confound him. The question is, did he kill her? If he did, the problem is Mr. Parker's and can be left to him. If he didn't, we are—"

The phone rang, and I swiveled and got it. "Nero Wolfe's resi—"

"Lon, Archie. I'm surprised you're there."

"Shouldn't I be?"

"Of course not. With your sidekick in the jug?"

"You're ahead of me. I spent the afternoon at a poetry reading and just got here."

"You're saying you didn't know that Orrie Cather has been pulled in on the Isabel Kerr murder?"

"Really?"

"Yep, really. If it would help to have something in print, I'm always available. I don't expect you to show me Wolfe's hole card, but if there's some little item . . ."

"Sure. Certainly. Of course. The minute I have something hot, or even warm, I'll ring you. Right now I'm busy. I'm telling Mr. Wolfe about a beautiful poem a man read."

"I'll bet you are. Just enough for a paragraph?"

"At the moment, no. Not on Sunday. Thanks for calling."

I hung up, swiveled, and told Wolfe, "Lon Cohen fishing, probably from home, since it's Sunday. An item in the *Gazette* tomorrow will start: 'Orrie Cather, a private detective, trusted assistant of Nero Wolfe, is being held as a material witness in connection with the murder of Isabel Kerr. Mr. Cather, a free-lance operative, has been an important factor in the spectacular success of many of Nero Wolfe's famous cases. Archie Goodwin, who is merely Nero Wolfe's errand boy, told—'"

"Shut up!"

I hunched my shoulders and raised my hands, palms up.

He slapped his desk blotter so hard the bottle trembled, and bellowed. "Did he kill her?"

I said firmly, "I pass."

"That won't do. When you were with him Friday evening was he planning murder? When you saw him yesterday was he bearing guilt?"

"I still pass. As for Friday evening, he may not have planned it. He may have gone there yesterday morning, no telling why, and flapped. As for yesterday afternoon, what do you mean, bearing guilt? Murderers have sat here in this room and looked you in the eye and answered your questions, and when they left you were still guessing. Now I'm guessing. Of course you want a verdict, but I haven't got it."

"You like to give odds. What are the odds?"

"For a bet, even money, and I'll take either end. That's ignoring my personal preference. I would prefer it that he didn't. I would rather not see a headline, NERO WOLFE'S ASSISTANT CONVICTED OF HOMICIDE—and so would you. People who read only headlines might think it was me."

"You refuse to resolve it."

"I do."

"Then get Saul and Fred here as soon as possible."

effective distress. If Orrie killed that woman to pro-
self her from interfering with his private plans, I am

3

At a quarter to ten Wolfe was making a speech.

Saul Panzer, five feet seven, 145 pounds, big nose
and flat ears, hair the color of rust but not rusty,
was in the red leather chair with a bottle of Mon-
trachet 1958 on the stand and a glass with a stem in
his hand. Fred Durkin, five feet ten, 190 pounds, bald
and burly, was on one of the yellow chairs facing
Wolfe's desk, with a bottle of Canadian and a pitcher
of water handy. He hadn't touched the water. I had
no refreshment. Fritz had been gone since early afternoon on his own affairs, and Wolfe and I had helped
ourselves around seven o'clock, concentrating mainly
on a block of headcheese. I have spent a total of at
least ten hours watching Fritz make headcheese, trying to find out why it is so much better than any
other I have ever tasted, including what my mother
used to make out in Ohio, but finally I gave up. It
could be the way he holds the spoon when he skims.

Saul and Fred had been thoroughly briefed on the
situation, except for one item, the name of the man
who had rescued Isabel Kerr from show business. Orrie wouldn't have liked that, but he had told Parker
that he wanted me to decide how to handle it, and if
they were going to vote they had to know the facts.
The name of the fairy godfather didn't matter. When
they had asked a few questions and had been answered, Wolfe started his speech.

"It is not merely a question," he said, "of devising an

effective defense. If Orrie killed that woman to prevent her from interfering with his private plans, I am not obliged to thwart the agents of justice and neither are you. Sympathy with misfortune, certainly, but not contravention of Nemesis. Mr. Parker is a competent lawyer, and it can be left to him. But if he didn't kill her I have an obligation I can't ignore. I am constrained not only by his long association with me but also by my self-esteem. You must know that I have no affection for him; he has frequently vexed me; he has not the dignity of a man who has found his place and occupies it, as you have, Fred; nor the integrity of one who knows his superiority but restricts it to areas that are acceptable to him, as you have, Saul. But if he didn't kill that woman, I intend to deliver him."

He turned a palm up. "The question is, did he? Having no firm opinion of my own, and no basis for one, I asked Archie. I thought he would at least have odds, one way or the other. He always has odds, but he failed me. He said that for a bet it was even money. Archie? That was four hours ago. Now?"

I shook my head. "I still pass. Damn it, go ahead and start something and see what we get!"

"No. We would be committed and make mistakes. Fred. You have known Orrie longer than I have. The situation has been fully described to you. What do you say?"

"Jesus," Fred said.

"That doesn't help. He would merely tell him to go and sin no more. Did he kill her?"

Fred put his glass down and shifted in his chair. He looked at Saul, then at me, and back at Wolfe. "It's too tough," he said. "Have I got it straight? If we decide he killed her you lay off and it's up to Parker. If we decide he didn't, you try to prove it, and of course the only way to prove it would be to find out who did and nail him. Is that it?"

"Yes."

"Then I say he didn't."

"Is that your considered opinion?"

"To be honest, no. The only way I could be sure he killed her would be if he confessed, and Orrie never would. But we know Orrie. He has always done whatever he felt like with women, and they let him. I mean they couldn't help it. But now apparently it's hit him and he wants to get hitched. So if this Isabel Kerr got in his way, really blocked him . . . well, I don't know. I mean I think I really do know. But you called us in to help you decide, didn't you?"

"Yes."

"Then I say no. He didn't."

Wolfe didn't even frown at him. Such a contribution from me would have got what I deserved, but he knows how Fred's mind works, and he had asked for it. He merely said, "That is hardly decisive," and turned his head. "Saul?"

"No," Saul said. "To put it the way Archie would, one will get you twenty that he didn't kill her."

"Indeed." Wolfe was surprised. "An opinion, or a gesture?"

"Call it a conclusion. Make it fifty to one. I'm not saying I'm superior to Archie. Since he knows everything I know, you may wonder why he didn't settle it, but that's obvious. He couldn't see it because he's involved personally. He's not conceited enough."

"Pfui. This is flummery."

"No, sir. I'll spell it out. First, say Orrie planned it. When he was with Archie, Friday evening, he intended to go there in the morning and kill her, and when Archie went in the afternoon, with gloves and keys, he would either find the body or, if someone had beat him to it, he would find police cars outside and a flock of cops inside. That's absolutely impossible. I don't know if you know it, but Orrie regards Archie as the smartest and quickest performer around. There's not the slightest chance that he would deliberately arrange to sit facing him and frame that kind of a deal. Anyway, why? If he was going to kill her, why such a flimflam with Archie?"

"All right, cross it off," I said. "I already had. Friday evening he wasn't even intending to see her, let alone kill her. But what if he decided to go, no matter why, Saturday morning? And she stung him."

Saul nodded. "And he killed her. Okay. Whether he stays to frisk the place for the objects he wants, or he doesn't, he goes back to his tailing job. He has a tough decision to make, whether to ring you and tell you not to go, with some kind of a reason. I admit he might not be able to cook up a good enough reason and he might decide it was too risky, it would be better to let you go. But now here's the point, the big point. You know him, and so do I. We know exactly how his mind works. You heard me ask Mr. Wolfe if there were any phone calls for you yesterday afternoon between four-thirty and six-thirty, and he said no. That's what settles it."

"Good. Wonderful."

"It's perfectly simple. You didn't see it because you were personally involved. Here's Orrie on his tailing job with the murder behind him. He decides not to call you off. He knows that when you go there and find the body you'll wonder about him. He knows that you think he'll be holding his breath, waiting to hear what objects you found and got. He knows that if he hadn't gone there and killed her, if she was still alive as far as he knew, he would be damned anxious to learn how you had made out, say from five-thirty on, and he would have called you. Therefore he *would* call you. But he didn't. That's the point."

"Back up," I said. "You can't have it both ways. If he didn't kill her, why didn't he call?"

"He would have, probably soon after he got home, but you rang him first. If he had killed her he wouldn't have waited until he got home. As you know, his worst fault is that he pushes. He knew that the natural thing would be for him to call, and, pushing it, if he had killed her, he would probably have called around five o'clock. Certainly by five-thirty. Damn it, he's not some stranger we can only guess about; we know him like a book."

He turned to Wolfe. "Since you and Archie are passing and Fred is yes and no, my vote tips it. If you buy that and take it on, and want to use me, it will be on me, including expenses. I have no more affection for Orrie than you have, but of course I would want to back up my vote."

"Me too," Fred blurted. "I voted no."

That was quite an offer. Saul, who asks ten dollars an hour and gets it, could afford it, but Fred doesn't rate that high and he has a wife and four children.

Wolfe's eyes came to me, and I met them. "The trouble is," I said, "I'm personally involved. It depends partly on how smart and quick Orrie thinks I am, and that cramps me. But it also depends on how smart I think Saul is, and I would hate to embarrass him either way. I'll switch and vote no, but I'm not giving any twenty to one."

He drew in a bushel of air through his nose, held it three seconds, and let it out through his open mouth. He screwed his head around to look at the wall clock, curled his fingers over the ends of the chair arms, and said, "Grrrhhhh." It was hard to take. A month of the new year had passed with no new business, and he was going to have to work for nothing.

He looked at Saul. "When can you start?"

"Now," Saul said.

"You, Fred?"

"Tuesday," Fred said. "I'm on a little job, but I can clean it up tomorrow."

Wolfe grunted. "You know the situation. We have nothing. We have never had less. We don't even know what objects the police found, if any, involving Orrie. On that Mr. Parker may help. Archie. Are they infesting that neighborhood?"

"Certainly. Of course they're concentrating on Orrie, trying to find someone who saw him yesterday morning. For a case, they need to get him there."

He turned to Saul. "We'll have to begin with banality. Who are the other tenants of the building? Who was seen entering or leaving yesterday morning? Did anyone see Archie enter or leave yesterday afternoon? That might become an issue. You will start on that tomorrow, and Fred will join you on Tuesday, but you will call twice a day to ask if something better has been suggested." He turned to me. "You will see someone. Who?"

I took five seconds. "Jill Hardy, if she's available. She may be in Rome. Or Tokyo."

"In that case, the sister? Mrs. Fleming?"

"Maybe, but I like Jill Hardy better. Do you want her?"

He made a face. "Only if you think I must." He pushed his chair back and pried himself up. "Confound it, I'm going to bed. I appreciate your offer, Saul, and yours, Fred, but this undertaking is mine. Your usual rates, and of course expenses. Good night."

He headed for the door.

4

As I sat in the kitchen at ten minutes past eight Monday morning, having brioches, grilled ham, and grape thyme jelly, my mind was hopping around.

First, why was Fritz so damn stubborn about the jelly? Why wouldn't he try it, just once, with half as much sugar and twice as much sauterne? I had been at him for years.

Second, why were journalists so damn lazy? If the *Times* felt it had to decorate the follow-up on the murder with a picture, surely they could have scared up one of Orrie, but they had the nerve to run that eight-year-old shot of Nero Wolfe. He ought to sue them for invasion of privacy. He hadn't been pinched. As far as they knew he wasn't in it at all. Of course it might not be laziness; maybe they were still sore about a letter he had once written the food editor.

Third, should I buzz him, or go up, before leaving? Fritz had had no word for me when he came down from taking up his breakfast tray, so apparently I was to proceed as instructed, but it wouldn't hurt to check.

Fourth, where was Jill Hardy? Orrie had told me she was with Pan Am, but it would take more than a phone call to get her address out of them. I had tried the phone books of all five boroughs last night; no Jill Hardy. Parker could get it when he saw Orrie, but that would mean waiting. I would be ready to go when I finished the second cup of coffee, and the sooner I—

The phone rang. Fritz started to come; he agrees with Wolfe that nothing and no one should be allowed to interrupt a meal; but I reached and got it. "Nero Wolfe's office, Archie Goodwin speaking."

"Oh! I—This *is* Archie Goodwin?"

"Right."

"The Archie Goodwin who works for Nero Wolfe?"

"I must be, since you called Nero Wolfe's number."

"Of course. My name is Jill Hardy. You probably— you may have heard it." Her voice was what Lily Rowan calls mezzotinto, good and full but with sharp edges.

"Yes, I believe I have."

"From Orrie Cather."

"Right."

"Then you know who I am. I'm calling—I have just seen the morning paper. Is it true about Orrie? He has been *arrested?*"

"You can call it that, yes. He is being held as a material witness. That means that the police think he knows things he hasn't told them, and they want him to."

"About a *murder?*"

"Apparently."

"They must be crazy!"

"That's quite possible. Are you at home, Miss Hardy?"

"Yes, at my apartment. Do you know—"

"Hold it, please. Since you say you just saw it in the paper, I assume the police haven't paid you a call yet. But they will. At least, they may. I need to ask a question. I sort of gathered from things Orrie said that you and he are planning to get married. I might have misunderstood. . . ."

"You didn't. We're going to be married in May."

"Is it known? Have you told people?"

"I have told a few people—friends. I'm going to

go on working for a while, and an airline stewardess is not allowed—"

"I know. But if Orrie has told his friends, and he told me, you'll have callers before long. If you want to have—"

"I want to know why he was arrested! I want to know—was he working for Nero Wolfe?"

"No. He hasn't been on a job for Mr. Wolfe for more than two months. If you—"

"Why should *I* have callers?"

"I'd rather not tell you on the phone. It's complicated. If you want to know about it before the police come to ask questions, why don't you come and ask me questions? Nero Wolfe's office, Nine-thirty-eight West Thirty-fifth Street. I'll be—"

"I can't. I'm due for a Rio flight at ten-thirty."

"Then I'll come and pick you up and we can talk on the way to the airport. I'm a good driver. What's the address?"

"I don't think—" Silence. "What if Orrie—" More silence. "I'll see." She hung up.

I had room for another brioche and slice of ham, and I didn't dawdle. It might take her only a couple of minutes. When Fritz brought coffee I told him that when you wanted to see someone and didn't know where she was all you had to do was send out waves, and he asked if we had a client.

"Yes and no," I said. "A job for someone, yes. A customer who can be properly billed, no. You heard me mention Orrie's name, so you might as well know that he's in a hole and we're going to pull him out. How do you say in French 'the brotherhood of man'?"

"There is no such thing in French. So that's what your personal errand was Saturday. I'm glad it's Orrie instead of Saul or Fred, but all the same—"

The phone rang. I got it. "Nero Wolfe's office—"

"Jill Hardy again, Mr. Goodwin. I've fixed it. I'll be there in about an hour."

"Good for you. Do you mind giving me your address and phone number? Just to have."

She didn't mind. The address was 217 Nutmeg Street, in the Village. When I had finished the coffee and went to the office, I wrote it on a slip of paper, and the phone number, and considered a problem: should it go in Orrie's folder? Deciding against it, I got out a new folder and marked it CATHER, ORRIE, CLIENT. In ten minutes Wolfe would be taking the elevator for his morning session, nine to eleven, with the orchids, and I buzzed his room on the house phone. He took his time to answer.

"Yes?"

"Good morning. I thought you would want to know that it's possible that Jill Hardy will still be here when you come down. She'll arrive in about an hour, probably less."

"You have already found her?"

"Oh, sure. It's easy when you know how."

"Swagger," he said, and hung up.

As I dusted desks and chairs, removed yesterday's sheets from the desk calendars, changed the water in the vase on Wolfe's desk, and opened the mail, I decided that Jill Hardy would be tall and stiff with quick, sharp eyes, the sergeant type, but the corners of her eyes would slant up a little because some Oriental had got mixed in somewhere along the line. It would have taken something unusual like that to hook Orrie so hard, but there was another reason why she had to be like that. Since we had ruled Orrie out, the sooner we found a replacement for him the better, and of course Jill Hardy was a candidate, and it would simplify it if she looked the part.

Damn it, she didn't. When the doorbell rang a little after nine-thirty and I went to the hall and to the front door, what I saw through the one-way glass was a size twelve black leather coat with a fur collar, and a little oval face, pink from the cold, with big gray-blue eyes, under a fur-and-leather pancake. When I had opened up and she was inside and the coat was off, she looked even smaller in the well-fitted dark blue suit. She must have just barely hit the minimum height for her job. In the office, I had one of the yellow chairs in place for her. The red leather chair is too far away from my desk.

"I've calmed down a little," she said as she sat. "You look a little like Orrie. The same size."

That didn't strike me as an ideal opening for a friendly conversation. I do not look like Orrie. He's handsome and I'm not. My face needs more nose, but I quit worrying about it when I was twelve. I turned the other cheek. "I'm not surprised," I said, "that Orrie decided to merge. Seeing you. I'll congratulate him again when I see him."

She ignored the oil. "When will you see him?"

"I'm not sure. Possibly this afternoon."

"I want to see him, but I don't know how. What do I do?"

"I wouldn't try to rush it if I were you. He might get bailed out. He has a good lawyer. When did you see him last?"

"Why did they *arrest* him?" she demanded. "What could he know about a *murder*? You say he wasn't working for Nero Wolfe?"

"Yes. He wasn't. I don't know, Miss Hardy, if I can tell you much of anything you don't already know, since you've read the paper. I suppose that woman, Isabel Kerr, was involved in some case he was working on, but that's just a guess. Another guess is that he was in her apartment recently, and they found his fingerprints there, and that's why they've got him. You probably know that private detectives sometimes get into a place and make a search, but if it had been that, Orrie wouldn't have left any prints because he would have had gloves on. Of course he might not have been there on business, it might have been just—social. Do you know if he knew Miss Kerr?"

"No." She was frowning.

"He has never mentioned her name?"

"No."

"When did you see him last?"

She was tops at ignoring questions. She was still frowning. "You said you'd rather not tell me on the phone why I would have callers, but you're not telling me anything, it seems to me. You're Orrie's close friend, but you don't seem to know much. Why would I have callers? You mean the police?"

I decided I wasn't going to get anywhere walking on eggs. "I don't want to jolt you," I said, "but I think you ought to know the situation."

"So do I. That's exactly what I think."

"Fine. When a man is arrested he has a right to call a lawyer. Orrie called Nathaniel Parker, and Parker went and saw him, and then he came here and talked with Mr. Wolfe and me. Orrie knew he was going to. They don't hold a man without bail *morely* because they think he knows things. They're holding him because they think he killed Isabel Kerr. They don't just think he knows something about a murder, they think he did it."

Her eyes were wide, staring. "I don't believe it."

"If you don't believe he did it, neither do I. If you don't believe they think he did, ask them. Or his lawyer. Because Mr. Wolfe doesn't think he did, he intends to do something about it, like for instance finding out who did. I haven't answered your question, why you should expect callers. Because as soon as the cops find out that Orrie is going to marry you, which won't take them long, they will want to ask you things. Like what I asked, do you know if he knew Isabel Kerr, and like what you haven't answered, when did you see him last? I only asked it twice, but they'll bear down. They'll also want to know where and how you spent Saturday morning; that's the kind of minds they have. They will wonder if you were there with him, and maybe even held her while he got the ashtray. It's also the kind of mind I have. Since I think he didn't kill her I have to consider who did, and it might have been you. Where were you Saturday morning?"

Her jaw was working. "I thought you were a *friend* of Orrie's," she said. "You wouldn't talk like that if he was here."

"Yes I would, and he would understand. He wouldn't like it, but he would understand." I leaned to her, elbows on knees. "Listen, Miss Hardy. I like your looks and I like your voice. You have very nice hands. You say you had never heard of Isabel Kerr, and I have no evidence that you had, so apparently you're out, but I would really appreciate it if you would tell me when you saw Orrie last and where you were Saturday morning."

"*Why* do they think he killed her?" she demanded. "Why *would* he kill her?"

"I don't know. I may have an idea later, possibly this afternoon if I see him, from the questions they have asked him. They probably think they have some line on motive, but not necessarily."

"How *could* he have a motive?"

"You'll have to ask them, not me, because I think they're off. It's supposed to be possible to convict a man of murder without proving motive, but juries don't like the idea."

"*Juries?* You mean they will—there'll be a *trial?*"

"I sincerely hope not."

Her eyes were fastened on me. "I believe you really mean that."

"I really do."

"Saturday morning I was at home in bed, until after noon. I had been on a flight from Caracas that was due at midnight, but we weren't down until after two o'clock. I saw Orrie that evening. I had dinner with him at a restaurant. I have to answer so many questions in the air that when I'm on the ground I don't listen to them." She pulled her feet back, stood up, and took a step. "Get up and put your arms around me."

It was an order, and I obeyed. She didn't lift her arms so we could lock, but when I had her enclosed she gripped my jacket with both hands near my backbone and hid her face on my chest. The dark blue suit felt like wool, but nowadays you never know. I didn't squeeze, just held her nice and firm, trying to decide whether she knew she was in trouble and wanted to enlist me, or she was getting started on me in case Orrie got permanently eliminated, or it was just a habit she had. She hadn't used any perfume, or very little, and she smelled fine. There's no telling how long it would have lasted if it hadn't been for the doorbell. It rang.

I unwound my arms, politely, crossed to the hall and took a look, stepped back in, and told her, "It's a cop, one I happen to know. Since you're in no hurry to meet him, you will please duck." I had crossed to the door to the front room and opened it. "In here. You don't have to hold your breath, it's soundproofed. You can even sneeze."

Generally speaking, airline stewardesses know how to react. Without a word she picked up her handbag, which had dropped to the floor when she gripped my jacket, moved to the door I was holding, and on through. As I shut the door the doorbell rang. I broke no records getting to the hall and the front; and if Inspector Cramer noticed the black leather coat on the rack, let him. It was me he wanted to see, since he knew Wolfe was never available until eleven, and one more question to refuse to answer wouldn't matter. I opened the door, said, "Sorry, I was busy yawning," and gave him room. His big round face was redder than usual from the cold. There have been times when he refused help with his coat because he wanted to get his eyes on me and keep them there, but now he let me behind him to take it, and he led the way to the office. He hadn't noticed the black leather coat, but he did notice the yellow chair near my desk, and as he lowered his broad rump onto the red leather one he asked, "Company?"

I nodded. "Come and gone. Have you turned Orrie loose yet?"

"No. Not yet and not soon. Unless you can give me a damn good reason. Can you?"

"Sure. He's clean."

"Go right ahead."

"Parker came here after seeing him yesterday and told us that Orrie had told him he was innocent. We have seen a lot of Orrie and we know he's not a liar. So Mr. Wolfe is going to look into it. Of course that's what you came for, to ask if he's going to horn in. He is."

"I don't have to ask that. I came to get information." He got better arranged in the chair. "When did you see Cather last?"

I shook my head. "No comment."

"Has he ever spoken to you about Isabel Kerr?"

"Pass."

"Has he ever spoken to you about Jill Hardy?"

"No comment."

"You can't get away with it, Goodwin. If a man is charged he can clam up, but you're not charged. But, by God, you can *be* charged."

"I feel another yawn coming," I said. "Do we have to go through it again? I don't say I will answer no questions at all about Orrie Cather. If you ask me where he buys his shoes or when did Mr. Wolfe last use him on a job, I'll tell you, even in writing. But the kind of questions you're loaded with, no. Certainly, if you pin a murder on him and make it stick, and if you can prove that I had information that you could have used, you can tag me for obstructing justice and I'll be sunk. But if it turns out that instead of obstructing justice I'm doing it a favor by helping Mr. Wolfe find out who *did* kill

Isabel Kerr, he and I ought to get a ticker-tape parade, but we won't insist on it."

He opened his tight lips to say, "You've crawled out on that limb before."

"Yeah. I said do we have to go through it again." I glanced at my wrist. "Mr. Wolfe will be down in twenty minutes, if you think you can scare him better than me."

He started tapping the floor with the toe of his heavy shoe, focusing on Wolfe's empty chair. That wasn't very satisfactory, since it made no sound on the thick rug, not like the linoleum in his office. He was looking at the chair instead of me because it wasn't my stand that was eating him. He had the answer to one question, where did Wolfe stand, and now the point was, why? Did we really have something, and, if so, what?

"It occurs to me," I said, "that we might make a deal. It would have to be okayed by Mr. Wolfe, but I'm sure he would. We'll make an affidavit, the last sentence of which will say that it includes everything we know, and everything Orrie has said and done to our knowledge, that could possibly have any bearing on the murder, and we'll trade it for a look at your file. The *whole* file. It would be a bargain for both of us. You would know exactly what we've got, and we would know why you're risking holding him without bail. Fair enough?"

"Balls," Cramer said. He stood up. "One thing I came for, to tell Wolfe something, but you can tell him. Tell him that it's too bad I can't show him Isabel Kerr's diary. If he read it he would change his mind about horning in. And a tip for you. When you decide to kill someone make damn sure he isn't keeping a diary. Or she." He turned and marched out.

I stayed put. It would have been a shame to spoil such a good exit line. When I heard the front door open and close I went to the hall for a look, to see that he had been outside when he shut it, then stepped back into the office and considered a matter. Should Jill Hardy be there in the red leather chair when Wolfe came down? If I left her in the front room and reported, almost certainly he would refuse to see her, and of course he should. It would be eleven o'clock in three minutes. I decided to bring her in, went and opened the door and crossed the sill, and looked around at an empty room. She had exited without a line, by the door to the hall. I went and looked at the rack; her coat was gone. The house phone buzzed in the office, and I went and got it. It was Wolfe, in the plant rooms, wanting to know if she had gone, and I told him yes, and in a minute the sound came of the elevator grumbling its way down. He entered, in his hand the daily orchids for his desk—a panicle of *Odontoglossum hellemense*, which, according to the records I keep, is a cross of harvengtense and crispum. A stunner if you feel like orchids, which I didn't just then. I sat and simmered as he put them in the vase, got settled in his chair, and glanced through the mail. When he finished with a letter from a man upstate who sends deer meat, the only important item, I said, rather loud, "Miss Kerr kept a diary."

He put the letter down, looked up, regarded me for half a minute, and asked, "How did you pry it out of him?"

"Out of who?"

"Mr. Cramer, of course."

I stared. "To see the street from up there you have to stick your head way out."

"I never have. But he would certainly come, and soon, and who else could supply such a particular? How did you pry it out of him?"

"All right, I'll report." I did so, starting with Jill Hardy. Sometimes, reporting a conversation, it's essential to give it verbatim, but even when it isn't I do it anyway because that's how I have trained and it's easier. As usual, he leaned back with his eyes closed. I went right on through, from Jill Hardy on to Cramer, since there had been no break, just a change of cast. When I finished he opened his eyes halfway, closed them again, and muttered, "Nothing."

"Right," I agreed. "As for her, if she's a liar she's pretty good. Orrie certainly thinks she knows nothing about Isabel Kerr, and if she does it would take a lot of digging to prove it. If she doesn't she's crossed off completely and is absolutely useless. As for Cramer, he probably has got a diary, but so what, we knew he had something hot, and I doubt if it says at the end, 'He is reaching for the ashtray and is going to hit me with it,' which is the point. Cramer may have needed a diary to tell him that it would be handy for Orrie if she died, but we don't, we already knew it. What we need is somebody else it is handy for. It is for Jill Hardy, in a way, but I doubt if she knew it. As you say, nothing."

He opened his eyes. "You think Orrie killed her."

"No. I have looked over Saul's point, from all angles, and I like it. At the very least it packs a reasonable doubt, which is enough for a jury, so it will do for me. Anyhow, we're now on record. With Cramer. If it turns out that Orrie did it I'll never forgive him. I'll cop his girl. She already thinks I look like him."

He grunted. "Now what? Who?"

"I suppose the sister. Or Avery Ballou."

"We would have to discuss Mr. Ballou. The sister first." He straightened up and reached for *Invitation to an Inquest*.

5

There was a Barry Fleming in the Bronx phone book—address, 2938 Humboldt Avenue. Of course I didn't dial the number. According to the *Times*, she wasn't talking to reporters, and naturally she would think I was trying a dodge. I consulted the Bronx street guide to locate Humboldt Avenue, then grinned at myself as my hand went automatically to a pocket for my keyfold. Because of a regrettable occurrence some years back, I had made it a hard and fast rule never to go on an errand connected with a murder without a gun, and the rules you make yourself are the hardest to break, but there's a limit. Sororicide is by no means unheard of, but to suppose that Stella Fleming might have killed her sister, and therefore anyone who got in her reach should be ready to shoot, would be over-doing it, at least until I had a look at her. I returned the keyfold to my pocket, told Wolfe not to expect me for lunch, and left. After descending the stoop to the sidewalk I turned up my collar, even for the short stretch around the corner to the garage. Instead of a January thaw we were having a good long freeze, and the wind was doing its best to help.

It was twenty past twelve when I left the Heron in a parking lot and walked a block and a half to Number 2938, which was a regulation ten-story brick hive, to be found in all five boroughs, but especially the

Bronx. Of course it might not be the right Barry Fleming, but I would soon find out. The tiled floor of the lobby had a rubber runner, no rugs. There was no doorman, but the elevator man was there, a pasty-faced bozo in a uniform that was past due for the cleaner and presser, leaning against the wall. I advanced and said, "Fleming, please."

He shook his head and said, "There's nobody there."

"I know," I said, "that Mrs. Fleming isn't receiving any strangers, but I'm not a newspaperman. I want to discuss a personal matter with her, and I'm sure she would want to." In his case, the face *was* the index of the mind. He wasn't impressed and wasn't going to be. The only question was how much. I removed my gloves, got out my case and extracted a card, got out my wallet and extracted a finif, and said, "On the level. Do you want to see my license? Take me up, and if she doesn't let me in I'll double this."

He took the card and looked it over, took the bill and stuck it in a pocket, and said, "On the level, there's nobody there. She went out around ten o'clock."

He deserved a good poke, but it wouldn't have been tactful. I merely asked, "Do you know where she went?"

He shook his head. "No idea."

"Do you know when she'll be back?"

"No, I don't."

I gave him a friendly smile. "That's not fifty cents' worth, let alone five bucks'." I got my wallet again and took out a ten. "What floor is she on?"

"Seven. Seven D."

"I need to see her, and she needs to see me. Take me up, and I'll wait there. You have my card. If you want to, get an inkpad and take my fingerprints."

He surprised me. He had a heart in him somewhere. He actually said, "She might be gone all day, and there's no place to sit."

"There's always the floor."

He gave me his eyes, looked straight at me for the first time. "No funny business, mister. The doors have got pretty good locks."

"I don't know anything about locks. There's nothing there for me until she comes." I went to the elevator and pressed my fingertips, all ten, against the metal frame, at eye level. "There. You've got me." I offered the sawbuck. He took it, followed me into the elevator, shut the door, and pushed the handle.

There are a lot of interesting things to do while you're waiting in an upper hall of an apartment house for four hours and twenty minutes. You can count spots and decide which has more, the left wall or the right wall. You can try to sort out smells and decide how many different flavors there are in the over-all effect. You can listen to the wails coming through the door of 7B and decide whether the little lamb is male or female and how old it is, and what steps you would take if you were inside. When people arrive or leave you can look straight at them and notice which ones look back and which ones pretend they haven't seen you. When a hefty, broad-shouldered woman turns after inserting a key into the lock of 7C and asks, "Are you waiting for someone?" you can say pleasantly and distinctly, "Yes," and see how she reacts. On the whole, it was time well spent. My one regret was that I hadn't brought along a chocolate bar, five or six bananas, and a quart of milk.

I admit I frequently glanced at my watch. It was ten minutes to five when the elevator door opened and a man emerged. When he kept coming down the hall I assumed he was headed for E or F, but he stopped to face me and spoke.

"I understand you're waiting for my wife."

Of course I had to concede it. "Yes, sir, I am, if you're Barry Fleming."

"She won't see you. You're wasting your time. She won't see anybody."

I nodded. "I know, but I think she'll see me if she lets me explain why."

I sent a hand to my pocket for the case, but before I had a card out he said, "I know who you are. I should say, I have seen the card you gave the elevator man. *Are* you Archie Goodwin?"

"I am. In person. Look, Mr. Fleming, why not leave it to her? When she comes I'll tell her what I want to talk about, and it will be up to her. I won't insist, I'll just ask her."

"What *do* you want to talk about?"

I would have preferred to tell her, but a husband is a husband. "About a man," I said. "His name is Orrie Cather, and the police think he killed Isabel Kerr. He has worked off and on for Nero Wolfe, and Mr. Wolfe and I know him very well, and we don't think he did. You know I work for Nero Wolfe?"

"Of course."

"We are looking into it a little, and I would like very much to ask your wife if she can supply any information that might help. Naturally she wants the murderer of her sister caught and punished, but she wouldn't want it to be Orrie Cather if he's innocent. You wouldn't, would you?"

"Of course not." He was puckering his lips and frowning at me. He was about my height, narrow-shouldered and narrow-hipped, with a long face that showed the cheekbones. He went on, "I wouldn't want an innocent man punished for anything, certainly not for murder. But I doubt very much if my wife can give you any information that would help. She's not—she's taking it pretty hard."

"Sure. Believe me, I don't want to make it any harder for her."

"Well—where's your coat?"

"There." I pointed to it, on the floor by the wall.

"Get it. There's no sense in waiting out here." With a key ring in his hand, he went to the door of 7D. When I came with my coat he was holding

the door open and I entered. The foyer was about
the size of a pool table. He hung my coat in the
closet before he took his off, and as he was hanging
his up the door opened and a woman entered. At
sight of me she gawked a second, then whirled to
him.

"*Barry!* You let him in?"

From her tone I knew then and there that I had
had a break, him coming first.

"Now, dear." He put an arm across her shoulders
and kissed her on the cheek. "He only wants some
information, if we have any. He thinks—"

"We have no information for anybody! You know
that!"

I spoke up. "But you must have a preference,
Mrs. Fleming. If an innocent man is convicted of
murdering your sister, the trouble is that the guilty
man goes free. Do you want that?"

She focused up at me. Up, because she wasn't
more than an inch over five feet. "It's none of your
business what I want," she said, and meant it.

"No," I said, "but it's *your* business. I'm not a
newshound trying to get a headline, I'm a private
detective trying to dig up some facts. I already have
some. I know why you won't see reporters, why
you have no information for anybody. Because your
sister was a doxy, and you—"

"My sister was a what?"

"D,O,X,Y, doxy. I happen to like that better than
concubine or paramour or mistress. I don't—"

I stopped because I had to, to protect my face.
When a woman flies at you to claw, what you do
depends on the woman. If she has real tiger in her
you may even have to plug her, but with Stella
Fleming, with her short reach, all I had to do was
stiff-arm her, with my palm flat on her mouth. Then
the husband got her shoulders from behind and
pulled her back and told me, "You'd better go."

I was inclined to agree, but it was just as well

that Wolfe couldn't read my mind by short-wave because he thinks I understand women. She turned and drummed on his chest with her fists and squeaked, "I don't want him to go," and then calmly, no hurry, started to shed her coat. When he had it she told me, "Come on inside," perfectly polite, and headed through an archway. When he had the closet door shut he motioned me on, and I moved.

She had turned on lights and gone to a couch and sat and was biting her lip. I hadn't really seen her, too busy, and as I crossed to a nearby chair I noted that she resembled her sister not at all, with her brown hair and brown eyes and round filled-out face. As I approached she demanded, "Why did you say that?"

"To jar you." I sat. "I had to. Either that or—"

"I mean why do you lie like that about my sister?"

I shook my head. "That line is wasted with me, Mrs. Fleming. We both know it's not a lie, so skip it. It's not important, not to me. I only said it to—"

"Did you know my sister?"

"No. I had never heard of her until yesterday."

"Then how could you know . . ."

I gave her three seconds, but she let it hang. I flipped a hand. "It's obvious. A showgirl leaves—"

"She was an actress."

"Okay. An actress leaves the theater, takes a three-hundred-dollar apartment, has no job, eats well, dresses well, has a car, uses thirty-dollar perfume. Who wouldn't know? Who doesn't know? That's not important, not now. What's—"

"It is to me. It's the most important thing in the world."

"Now, dear," Fleming said. He was beside her on the couch.

"Well," I said, "if it's that important to you, that's what you want to talk about. Go ahead."

"She was twenty-eight years old. I'm thirty-one. She was only twenty-five when she . . . stopped work. She was six and I was nine when our mother died, and she was twelve and I was fifteen when our father died. That's why it's so important."

I nodded. "Certainly."

"You're not a newspaper reporter. William told me your name, but I don't remember."

"William's the elevator man," Fleming said.

To him: "Thank you." To her: "My name is Archie Goodwin. I'm a private detective, I work for Nero Wolfe, and I came—"

"You're a detective."

"Yes."

"Then you know about things. You said I wouldn't want the man that killed my sister to go free, and no, I wouldn't, but if he's arrested and there's a trial, no one is going to say about my sister what you said about her. If anyone said that at the trial it would be in the newspapers. If anyone is going to say that there mustn't be any trial. Even if he goes free. So you didn't know what I want."

That made the second woman in one day who didn't want a trial, though for a different reason. "I do now," I told her, "and from your standpoint there's no argument. I even agree with you, at least part way. You don't want a trial even if they get the right man. What I don't want is a trial of the wrong man, and that's what is going to happen unless someone stops it. Of course you read the papers."

"I read all of them."

"Naturally. Then you know they are holding a man named Orrie Cather and that he has worked for Nero Wolfe. Had you ever heard or seen that name before? Orrie Cather?"

"No."

"Are you sure? Didn't your sister ever mention him?"

"No. I'm sure she didn't."

"Mr. Wolfe and I know him very well. We do not believe he killed your sister. I don't say we know *all* about him. He may have had, he may have, some—uh—connections that we don't know about. I will even concede that he may have been the one who was paying the rent for your sister's apartment, and her other— You're shaking your head."

"She didn't shake her head," Fleming said.

"Sorry, I thought you did. Anyway, whether he was paying the rent or not, we do not believe he killed her, and that's why Mr. Wolfe sent me to see you. If they bring him to trial—you know what will happen. Everything they have found out about your sister will be on record. As you know, a jury is supposed to acquit a man if there's a reasonable doubt. We want to establish a reasonable doubt for the police so it won't get in a courtroom for a jury, and we thought you might help. You saw your sister fairly often, didn't you?"

"That's pretty clever," Fleming said. "But I must remind you that for my wife a trial of the right man might be just as bad as a trial of the wrong man. I don't agree with her, not at all, but Isabel was *her* sister."

"No," I said, "I'm not being clever. All we need is a reasonable doubt. For instance, what if we can show the police that there's another man, or woman, who had a good motive? Or what if they learn that Isabel told someone—it could be your wife—that someone had threatened to kill her? If and if and if. For our purpose, Mr. Wolfe's and mine, it doesn't have to be strong enough to charge him and try him, just the doubt. But even if they nailed him, his trial might not be as bad, for your wife, as Orrie Cather's trial is sure to be. We know something about the line they think they have on Orrie."

"What is it?"

"I can't tell you that. We got it in confidence."

He was squinting at me. "You know, Mr. Goodwin, I'm a mathematics teacher and I like problems. Since this is so close to us, though it's closer to my wife than to me, it isn't *just* a problem, but still my mind has the habit." He put a hand on his wife's knee. "You won't mind, dear, if I admit I would like to help with this problem. But I won't. I know how you feel. You do exactly what you want to do."

"Fair enough," I told him. And to her: "You saw your sister often, didn't you?"

She had put her hand on top of his. "Yes," she said.

"Once or twice a week?"

"Yes. Nearly always we had dinner together on Saturday and went to a show or a movie. My husband plays chess Saturday evenings."

"According to the newspaper, when you went there day before yesterday you got no answer to your ring and the superintendent let you in. Is that correct?"

"Yes."

"That was an important moment, when you entered the bedroom. I don't want to jar you again, Mrs. Fleming, I truly don't, but it's important. What was your first thought when you saw your sister's dead body there on the floor?"

"I didn't—it wasn't a thought."

"First there was the shock, of course. But when you saw the—when you realized she had been murdered, it would have been natural to have the thought *He killed her* or *She killed her*, something like that. That's why it's important; a first thought like that is often right. Who was the He or the She?"

"There wasn't any he or she. I didn't have any such thought."

"Are you sure? At a time like that your mind jerks around."

"I know it does, but I didn't have a thought such as that then or any other time, that *he* killed her or *she* killed her. I couldn't even try to guess who killed her. All I know is there mustn't be a trial."

"There will be a trial, of Orrie Cather, unless we

can find a way to stop it. Did your sister ever show you her diary?"

She frowned. "She didn't keep a diary."

"Yes, she did. The police have it. But since—"

"What does it say?"

"I don't know. I haven't seen it. Since—"

"She shouldn't have done that. That makes it worse. She didn't tell me. She must have kept it in that drawer she kept locked. Don't I have a right to it? Can't I make them give it to me?"

"Now now. You can later. If there's a trial it will be evidence. It's called an exhibit. Since you never saw it, we'll have to skip it. It looks pretty hopeless, because I don't know of anyone but you who can give me any information. Of course a good prospect would be the man who paid the rent for the apartment, and the car and the perfume and so on, but I don't know who he is. Do you?"

"No."

"That surprises me. I thought you would. You were close with your sister, weren't you?"

"Certainly I was."

"Then you must know who else was. Since you say you couldn't even try to guess who killed her, I'm not asking that, just who knew her well. Of course you have told the police."

"No, I haven't."

I raised a brow. "Are you refusing to talk to them too?"

"No, but I couldn't tell them much because I don't know. It was . . ." She stopped, shook her head, and turned to her husband. "You tell him, Barry."

He squeezed her hand. "You could almost say," he said, "that Isabel lived two lives. One of them was with my wife, her sister, and to a much less extent me. The other one was with her—well, call it her circle. My wife and I know very little about it, but we sort of understood that her friends were mostly from the world of the theater. You will realize that in the circumstances my wife preferred not to associate with them."

"It wasn't what I preferred," she corrected. "It was what *was*."

That helped a lot, another whole circle, but I might have expected it. "All right," I told her, "you can't give me names you don't know. Isn't there anyone, anyone at all, that you know and she knew?"

She shook her head. "Nobody."

"Dr. Gamm," Fleming said.

"Oh, of course," she said.

"Her doctor?" I asked.

Fleming nodded. "Ours too. An internist. He's— you might say—a friend of mine. He plays chess. When Isabel had a bad case of bronchitis a couple of years ago I—"

"Nearly three years ago," she said.

"Was it? I recommended him. He's a widower with two children. We have had him and Isabel here two or three evenings for bridge, but she wasn't very good at it."

"She was terrible," Stella Fleming said.

"No card sense," Fleming said. "His name is Theodore Gamm with two Ms. His office is on Seventy-eighth Street in Manhattan."

Presumably he was helping with the problem, and I fully appreciated it; at least, by gum, I had one name and address. I got my notebook out and wrote it down to show that I was on the ball.

"He can't tell you anything," she said, perfectly calm, but suddenly she was on her feet, trembling, her hands tight fists, her eyes hot. "Nobody can! They won't, they won't! Get out! Get *out!*"

Fleming, up too, had an arm across her shoulders, but she didn't know it. If I had sat tight she would probably have soon got organized again, but I hadn't had a bite since breakfast. I nodded at Fleming, and he nodded back, and I went to the foyer for my hat and coat and let myself out. As I entered the elevator, William said, "So you got in, huh?" and I said, "Thanks to you, pal, telling both of them I was there." Outside it was even colder, but the Heron started like an angel, as it damn well should, and I headed for the Grand Concourse.

When I entered the office, a little after half past six, Wolfe was at his desk, scowling at a document two inches thick—part of the transcript of the Rosenberg trial, which he had sent for after reading the first three chapters of *Invitation to an Inquest*. My desk was clean, no memos or messages about phone calls. I yanked a sheet from my pocket notebook and sat studying it until Wolfe cleared his throat, whereupon I rose and handed it to him.

"There," I said. "The name and address of the doctor who treated Isabel Kerr when she had bronchitis nearly three years ago."

He grunted. "And?"

"You'll appreciate it more if I lead up to it. I spent an hour with Mr. and Mrs. Barry Fleming. Now or after dinner?"

He looked at the clock. Thirty-five minutes to anchovy fritters. "Is it urgent?"

"Hell no."

"Then it can wait. Saul called twice. Nothing. Fred will join him in the morning. I rang Mr. Parker, and he came after lunch and I described the situation, everything relevant except the name of Avery Ballou. He telephoned later. He had seen Orrie, and he has arranged for you to see him in the morning at ten o'clock. He thinks it advisable."

"Has Orrie been charged? Homicide?"

"No."

"But no bail?"

"No. Mr. Parker doesn't wish to press it." He glanced at the sheet I had handed him. "What's this? Did this man kill her?"

"No, he cured her. I'm very proud of it. It's the crop."

"Pfui." He dropped it and resumed with the transcript.

Business is taboo at the dinner table, but crime and criminals aren't, and the Rosenberg case hogged the conversation all through the anchovy fritters, partridge in casserole with no olives in the sauce, cucumber mousse, and Creole curds and cream. Of course it was academic, since the Rosenbergs had been dead for years, but the young princes had been dead for five centuries, and Wolfe had once spent a week investigating that case, after which he removed More's *Utopia* from his bookshelves because More had framed Richard III.

He let up only when we were back in the office and had finished with coffee. He pushed the tray aside and asked if it had to be verbatim, and I said yes and proceeded. When I told about the deal with William he pursed his lips, not objecting, merely reacting to the fact that the fifteen bucks was down the drain, since we couldn't expect to bill Orrie. Then he leaned back and closed his eyes and quit reacting, as usual, until I had finished.

He opened his eyes and demanded, "You had no lunch? None at all?"

I shook my head. "If I had gone out it might have cost a C to get back up. William is a mooch."

He straightened up. "*Never* do that."

"It's good for me. I was nine ounces overweight. Do you comment or do I?"

"You."

I took half a minute. "First, did Stella kill her sister? Two to one she didn't. She—"

"Only two?"

"That's the best I'll give. The most important thing in the world, she said. If it's still that important when she's dead, what was it when she was alive? She left the rails twice in my presence. She just can't stand

it. If she went there Saturday morning and—do I
need to spell it?"

"No. Why two to one? Why not even or less?"

"Because, on the record, a woman kills her sister
only if she hates her or is afraid of her. Stella didn't.
She loved her and wanted to—well, save her. Make
it three to one. Anyway, even if she did it, she's
hopeless. Try and prove it. Even if we got enough
to satisfy us, Cramer and the DA would never buy
it, let alone a jury. So forget her. As for him, no
bet. He could have had an elegant motive, anybody
could, but as of now the only one visible is that
he killed her to stop his wife worrying about her,
which is a little far-fetched. One thing, though, why
did he let me in?"

"So she wouldn't encounter you in the hall."

"Possibly, but he could have ordered me out and
called a cop if he had to. It's just a comment; maybe
it was because he likes problems, or maybe he thought
it would be good for her. More than a comment, a
conclusion: if they're out, they have no idea who
is in. She said she couldn't even try to guess, and
I believe her. She's no good at covering. When
I pulled an obvious little dodge, saying that it might
have been Orrie who was paying the rent, it wasn't
only her expression, she actually shook her head.
Later she said she didn't know who, but she does.
What the hell, so do we."

"If Orrie was candid."

"He was. He had the lid off. For comments, I
have saved the best for the last. Isabel's other life.
The circle."

He grunted. "Yes."

"Yes what?"

"That expands it. That was to be expected, as
soon as you learned that her relations with her sister
were restricted. A woman who eats by sufferance,
without a contract, would of course prefer not to
eat alone. You laugh?"

"I do. Most men wouldn't put it all on eating. All right, so we have a circle too—as expected. Dozens, maybe hundreds. Godalmighty. I suggest again that we consider Avery Ballou."

"I am considering him. I wanted first—no matter. We'll discuss it in the morning after you see Orrie." He reached for the transcript.

6

Where you go to see a man in custody in Manhattan depends partly on why he's there. It can be a precinct station, a room in the City Prison, a room in the District Attorney's office, or the paddock. I don't know how many cops call it the paddock, but Sergeant Purley Stebbins does. It is a bare, smelly room about twelve yards long, split along the center by a steel grill which extends from the middle of a wide wooden counter up to the ceiling, and there are a dozen or so wooden chairs strung along each side of the counter, the same kind of chairs for the visitors and visitees. Democracy.

Seated on one of the chairs on the visitors' side at ten minutes past ten Tuesday morning, I was not chipper. I had supposed I would see Orrie in a room at the DA's office until Parker had phoned to say it would be the City Prison, and then I had taken it for granted it would be in a room. But I had been escorted to the paddock, and there I was, with four other visitors spread along the line, the nearest one, a middle-aged fat woman with red eyes, only seven feet away. I would have liked to think they were merely showing what they thought of Nero Wolfe and Archie Goodwin, but I didn't. They had decided that Orrie Cather was a murderer, though they hadn't charged him yet, and were taking no chances. Try to make them eat it.

A door opened in the back wall, the other side of

the grill and counter, and Orrie entered, cuffed, with a dick right behind. The dick steered him to a chair opposite me, watched him sit, said, "Fifteen minutes," and went back to the wall, where another dick was standing. My eyes and Orrie's met as well as they could through the grill. The rims of his were puffy. He had once admitted to me that he brushed his hair ten minutes every morning, but he hadn't that morning.

"It *could* be bugged," I said.

"I don't think so," he said. His cuffed hands were on the counter. "Too risky. Too big a stink."

"Well, all we can do is keep it low. Parker has told you that Mr. Wolfe and Saul and Fred and I have decided that you didn't kill her and we're on it."

"Yeah, I knew he'd have to. I'm not his Archie Goodwin, but even me he'd have to."

"I perfer to regard myself as my Archie Goodwin, but we won't go into that now. I have a couple of questions, but Parker says you wanted to see me. Well?"

"I want you to do me a favor, Archie, a big favor. I want you to see Jill Hardy and tell her—"

"I've already seen her. She came to the office yesterday morning, don't interrupt, and we had a talk. I didn't know how much you had told her about Isabel Kerr so I—"

"I have never told her anything about Isabel Kerr. She didn't know there *was* an Isabel Kerr. Goddammit, what did you tell her?"

"Same as you, nothing. Of course that's the favor you were going to ask, and it's already done. I told her that the cops thought you killed her, and we thought you didn't, and we were going to investigate, and we knew nothing about Isabel Kerr. Now I have—"

"You're wonderful, Archie. Wonderful."

"Put it in writing and I'll frame it. I have questions,

and we haven't much time. Have you opened up at all?"

"No. I'm a dummy."

"Stay that way. As you know, Parker agrees. What have they got? We know they got your license and the other objects, since you didn't get them and I didn't, and your prints, and her diary, but is that—"

"Her *diary?*"

"Yeah. You didn't know she kept one?"

"My God, no."

"She did, and they have it, so Cramer says. He didn't say what's in it. Probably you are, but we want your opinion on another point: would she put his name in it? The name I had to pry out of you."

"Oh." He looked at it a few seconds. "I see. That might be a point. I don't think she would. Of course she had the diary stashed, but even so I'm pretty sure she wouldn't. She was too cagey. It's more than just an opinion. I say no."

I looked at my wrist. Six minutes to go. "Now *the* question. How many people knew about you and her?"

"Nobody."

"Nuts. You can't know that."

"As far as I know, nobody. You've heard me blow, Archie, but you never heard me blow about her. After just a few times with her she scared me. I had had women cotton to me before, but she was hipped. I liked her all right, she was good all right, but she was hipped. After we got started we were never together anywhere except her place. She wanted it that way, and that suited me. But I completely misjudged her. I told her about meeting Jill, you know, just that I had met an airline stewardess, and then like a damn fool I thought I could ease her along to the idea that since I wasn't her only contact she couldn't expect to be my only contact. Then *I* got hipped, for the first time in my life. On Jill. And she—I've told you how she took it. She was absolutely going to marry me herself, for God's sake. I told her my income was about half of what he was spending on that setup, and she said just a room and bath would do us even after the baby came. That kind of crap. I don't for a minute believe there was going to be a baby, and even if there was, whose would it be? I'm answering your question. I told nobody about her, and I doubt if she told anyone about me."

"But she told you about other people, didn't she?"

"Some, yes. You know, just talk, sure."

"Which one of them killed her? Who had a reason to?"

He nodded. "Naturally I've thought about it. If she ever said a single damn thing about anyone that might give a hint I can't dig it up. I realize that there's only one way you can spring me, and God knows I wish I could give you a steer, but I swear I can't. Sure, she told me about people, men who made passes at her, women she liked and some she didn't like, but I have gone over it and over it and came up with nothing. I know you have to start somewhere, and that's the other thing, besides Jill, I wanted to tell you. The woman she liked best, and saw the most of, is a night-club singer named Julie Jaquette. Her real name is Amy Jackson. She was at the Ten Little Indians week before last and may still be there. She would probably be the best bet. Have you got anything yet? Anything at all?"

"No. Did you ever meet the sister, Stella Fleming?"

"No. Isabel talked about her. She said that when we were married not only would she be happy, her sister would be too. I was supposed to get a kick out of that, making two women happy at once."

"You should have. Did she ever mention—" I stopped because we were about to be interrupted. The dick was coming. He touched Orrie on the shoulder, which was unnecessary, and said time was up. I raised my voice. "What's your name?"

He looked down his nose at me. "*My* name?"

"Yes. Your personal name."

"My name is William Flanagan."

"Another William." I rose. "I'm going to report you for brutality. Mr. Cather is merely detained as a material witness. You didn't have to grab his shoulder." I turned and headed for the door, and the dick who had brought me in joined me as I reached for the knob.

William Flanagan hadn't stopped anything important; I had only been going to ask if Isabel had ever mentioned Dr. Gamm.

In the taxi, going uptown, I touched bottom. I had hoped to get some little lead out of Orrie, at least a glimmer, but as we turned west at 35th Street I realized that I was going over how he had looked and what he had said for indications about him, which was plain silly, since he was supposed to be definitely out. Of course the trouble was that the only way to get something out of your mind is to get something else in. The idea that Orrie might have conked Isabel Kerr with that ashtray had popped into my head as soon as I saw the dent in her skull, and it was going to stay there, no matter what, until I had an X or Y to substitute for Orrie; and after three days and nights there was still no X or Y anything like good enough. If you say, even so, I shouldn't have been considering Orrie because we had barred him, you're perfectly right but you don't know much.

To show how I was taking it, when I entered the office I did not open the top left drawer of my desk to get the pad on which I enter items for my weekly expense account. The $3.75 cab fare would be on me. Wolfe had told us the undertaking was his, but until we brought him something he would have nothing to undertake, and he had no corner in self-esteem. Since it was only a couple of minutes past eleven, he had just come down from the plant rooms and was taking a look at the mail. When he found there was nothing interesting, no checks and no lists from orchid collectors, he pushed it aside and said good morning. I said it wasn't, and to prove it gave him a verbatim report of my talk with Orrie, ending with the comment that he had better take on the next one himself, since I had got nowhere with the three I had tackled, Jill Hardy and the Flemings.

"Anyway," I said, "it's a man. I admit that Julie Jaquette would probably be too much for you, but she can wait until you have had a go at Avery Ballou."

He frowned. "Dr. Gamm."

I frowned back. "You can't put it off forever. As you know, I agree with you on jobs like divorce evidence, they're too grubby. Any job is apt to be if the main point is who has been, or is, or will be, sleeping with whom. But while it's true that Ballou was probably not paying her rent so he could read poetry to her, that presumably sex was a factor, that's not the main point and you can ignore it. You can pretend that he might have killed her because she snickered when he pronounced a word wrong."

His lips were tight. He breathed three times before he said, "Very well. Bring him."

I nodded. "Okay, but I don't know when or how. I looked him up a little last night. He is not only president of the Federal Holding Corporation, he's also a director of nine other big outfits. He has a house in Sixty-seventh Street, one at Rhinebeck, and one at Palm Beach. He's fifty-six years old. He has one married son and two married daughters. I would have to call the bank to learn the size of his stack, and we don't want to advertise that you have any curiosity about him, but it—"

"I said bring him."

"I heard you. I am explaining that it wouldn't be advisable to tell the receptionist at his office, and the underling she would pass me to, that a private detective named Nero Wolfe wants to consult him about a matter that is too confidential for any ears but his. Phoning would be even worse. Therefore I must arrange something, and Julie Jaquette will have to be postponed."

He grunted. "Any word from Saul?"

"He phoned at nine o'clock. Fred was with him and they were proceeding. He'll call around one."

"Pfui. A prodigy on a treadmill. Take him off. Give him Miss Jaquette. He will get names from her, and Fred will help with them." He reached for the mail. "Your notebook. This letter from that ass in Paris will have to be answered."

7

At four o'clock that afternoon I stood in the marble
lobby of a forty-story financial castle in Wall Street,
across from the row of elevators that were marked
"32-40." I was equipped. In my head was a picture
of Avery Ballou, acquired from a back number of
Fortune magazine at the New York Public Library,
and in my pocket was a card. It was like the card
I had given William the elevator man—my name in
the middle and Nero Wolfe's name and address
and phone number in smaller type at the bottom
—but I had added something. Typewritten below my
name was the information: "There was a diary in
the pink bedroom and the police have it." It filled the
space neatly.

I may have been overdoing it. It was conceivable
that not only Ballou's wife and family, but also some
of his friends, and even some of the Federal Holding Corporation personnel, knew how he had spent
some of his evenings. But it was likely that they
didn't. Some of the adjectives about him in *Fortune*
were "astute," "aloof," "conventional," and "scrupu-
lous." I don't swallow printed adjectives whole, but if
that batch was only half right it was going to be
ticklish. So I spent a hundred minutes down in the
lobby instead of going up to the thirty-fourth floor.
Anyhow it was better than the upstairs hall at 2938
Humboldt Avenue, especially from five o'clock on,
when every elevator unloaded a flock of wrens, a

pleasing sight. I know that the wrens who lay eggs
don't flock, but if they used elevators instead of wings
they would have to.

I had looked at my watch at 5:38, and it was two
minutes later that Avery Ballou showed. Of those who
had been with him in the elevator, one man stayed
with him as they went down the lobby, talking. I
followed, six steps back, hoping they would separate,
and they did, out on the sidewalk. The man went
toward Broadway, and Ballou just stood there. I approached, faced him, offered the card, and said,
"This will interest you, Mr. Ballou. Is there enough
light?"

For a second I thought he was going to snub it,
and so did he, but he looked at my face, the manly
honest face that had launched a thousand cards, took
it, tilted it for better light, and focused on it. I had
plenty of time to size him up. His dark gray coat
had set him back three Cs, possibly four, and his
dark gray hat around forty bucks. His head was the
right size for his big solid frame, and his face was
a little seamy but had no sag. It still didn't say when
he finished with the card, stuck it in his pocket, and
looked at me.

"Interest *me?*" he asked.

I nodded. "Of course this is no place to discuss it.
The best place for that is Nero Wolfe's office. He
knows even more than the police do about that pink
bedroom and about the man they're holding, and
about you. The best time would be now. That's really all I have to say, I'm just the messenger boy. But
you have to admit it was considerate of me not to
go up to the thirty-fourth floor and give somebody
that card to take in."

He turned his head, clear around—to see if there
was a cop handy? No. A Rolls-Royce town car had
pulled up and stopped, and the uniformed chauffeur
was getting out. Ballou turned back to me and asked,
"Where is it?"

"West Thirty-fifth Street. Nine-thirty-eight."

"Have you a car?"

"Not here."

"If you ride with me you'll keep your mouth shut."

"Right. I've said my piece."

He stepped to the Rolls and got in, and I followed, and the driver shut the door and got in behind the wheel. As we moved, Ballou told him we would make a stop and gave him the address. As we stopped for a light at the corner I was thinking that it was the first time I had ever delivered a murder suspect to the old brownstone in his own Rolls-Royce. The rest of the way, since we were not speaking, I concentrated on how it handled, and decided it was a little smoother than the Heron but not quite as fast on the take.

It was after six when we got there, so Wolfe would be down. While I am not as childish as he is about showing off, I like to do things right, so after attending to Ballou's hat and coat, and mine, in the hall, I went to the office door, stepped in, announced, "Mr. Ballou," and moved aside. He entered, stopped, glanced around, and asked, "Is this room bugged?"

"Confound it," Wolfe said, "it will soon be impossible to converse anywhere about anything. I can give you my word of honor that what we say will not be recorded, and do, but though I know what my word is worth, you don't." He pointed to the vase. "The microphone could even be in there, but it isn't."

Ballou had taken the card from his overcoat pocket and had it in his hand. He showed it. "What is this about a pink bedroom and a diary?"

Wolfe turned a hand over. "That's obvious. A device to get you here. But not bogus, factual. The bedroom is pink, as you know, since you have spent many hours in it; and Miss Kerr did keep a diary; and the police have it." He motioned at the red leather chair. "Please be seated; eyes are better at a level."

"I have never spent an hour in a pink bedroom."

"Then why are you here?"

"Because I know something of your reputation. I

know you are capable of elaborate maneuvers, and apparently you intended to involve me in one. I wanted to tell you, don't try it."

Wolfe shook his head. "No good, Mr. Ballou. The question is not whether I know of your association, over a three-year period, with Miss Kerr, nor is it what evidence I have at hand to support my knowledge. The question is, can public disclosure of it be prevented, and if so, how? That is the question for you. For me the question is, did you kill that woman? If you did, I'm going to establish it and you're doomed. If you didn't, I have no desire to expose your association with her, and it may never transpire. It is not overweening to say that that issue depends chiefly on how candid you are with me."

Ballou turned his head as I crossed behind him to my desk. He regarded me as I sat, looked at Wolfe, moved to the red leather chair, got himself comfortably seated, taking his time, and told Wolfe, "I'm listening."

Wolfe swiveled to have him straight front. "Some of this may be news to you, but some may not. You know, of course, that a man named Orrie Cather is in custody as a material witness, but he will be charged with homicide at any moment. I have assumed, on sufficient ground, that he is innocent. Mr. Cather has worked for me, on occasion, for years, and I am under an incumbency. If I am to satisfy it I must now violate a confidence. Mr. Cather had been on intimate terms with Miss Kerr for about a year. He visited her frequently at her apartment with the pink bedroom, at times when she knew you would not come, and there were traces there of his presence and the intimacy, not visible to you but discoverable by a search. The police found them, and that's why they have him. Do you wish to comment?"

"I'm listening." From Ballou's face you might have thought he was merely hearing a proposition to hold something.

"Miss Kerr told Mr. Cather many things about you,

her provider, but naturally did not tell you about him, her Strephon. Apparently she also put him in her diary, but not you. If you were there, you would have been visited before now by a policeman or the District Attorney. Have you been?"

"I'm listening."

"That won't do. I need to know, and it doesn't commit you. Has anyone called on you?"

"No."

"Have you had any indication whatever that your name might be a factor in the murder of Isabel Kerr?"

"No."

"Then it isn't in the diary. I know only one thing about the diary, that the police found it in Miss Kerr's apartment. A policeman, an inspector, told Mr. Goodwin that they had it. I know nothing of its contents except, now, that it doesn't name you, and that's fortunate. It's probable that the District Attorney will not charge Mr. Cather with murder until he learns who was paying for that apartment; that would be dictated by prudence. You hope he never learns, and I would be just as well satisfied."

Wolfe cocked his head. "That's the point, Mr. Ballou. If Mr. Cather is brought to trial, you're in for it. He will take the stand, he will speak, and he will certainly name you; and the dogs will be loose. There may be a chance, even a good one, that if the murderer in fact is exposed and tried, and convicted, your name will never be divulged; but if Mr. Cather is tried, it will inevitably be divulged. Assuming his innocence as I do, I don't want him to be tried, and neither do you, now that I have described the situation. We have a common interest, and I expect you to help me pursue it—to identify the man who killed Isabel Kerr. If you refuse, I shall of course assume that you killed her, and if you didn't I would waste much valuable time, and that would be a pity. Have I made it clear?"

Ballou's face looked seamier, but that was all;

there was still no sag. He took a deep breath, rubbed
his brow with a palm, and said, "Could I have a
drink?" I rose and said certainly, name it, because
that was quicker than ringing for Fritz, and he said
gin on the rocks with lemon peel, and I went to the
kitchen. Fritz shaved slivers of lemon peel while I
got the gin and a glass and a bowl of ice cubes.
When I re-entered the office the red leather chair
was empty; Ballou was over by the globe, slowly
twirling it with a fingertip. As I put the tray on the
stand he came, sat, put one ice cube in the glass,
poured gin, twisted two pieces of lemon peel and
dropped them in, and stirred. When I was back in
my chair he was still stirring. Finally he picked up
the glass, took two medium sips, and put it down.

"Yes," he said, "You have made it clear."

Wolfe opened his eyes and grunted.

"Obviously," Ballou said, "I'm in a trap. I can't
check a single thing you have said. I did want a
drink, I always have one as soon as I get home, but
what I had to have was a little time to consider. I
have decided that the probability is that the facts are
as you have given them, partly because I don't see
what you could possibly expect to gain by inventing
them. The only alternative is to walk out, and I can't
risk it. I have a question: when did Miss Kerr—when
did that man, Cather, first learn my name?"

Wolfe turned. "Do we know, Archie?"

"No, sir," To Ballou: "I can find out, if it's important."

"Could it have been as long as four months ago?"

"Certainly."

"I would like to know. It may not be important
now, but I would like to know." He got the glass
and took a sip. "I have nothing to say to your guess
that I killed Miss Kerr except that I didn't. Would
a man in my position, of my standing—No, that
wouldn't impress you. To me the idea is simply fan-
tastic. You say you expect me to help you identify
the man who killed her. If Cather didn't, and if

the facts are as you say, I certainly want to, but how?"

"First you," Wolfe said. "Where were you Saturday morning?"

"I was at home all morning and until about three o'clock. We had guests for lunch."

"If pressed, could you account for every half-hour from eight o'clock to noon?"

"I think so. There were phone calls."

"Could your wife?"

"Why the devil should she?"

Wolfe shook his head. "Don't start that. You have held your poise admirably; don't spoil it. I don't drag your wife in, circumstances do. Did she know of your association with Miss Kerr?"

"No."

"How sure are you?"

"Completely. I have taken great precautions."

Wolfe frowned. "You see how difficult it is. It may be highly desirable for Mr. Goodwin or me to see your wife, but with what excuse, without involving you? It must be managed somehow, and Mr. Goodwin—"

"It will *not* be managed! You will *not* see my wife!"

"Your poise. As you said, you're in a trap; don't thrash about. If it wasn't you or your wife, who was it? I must have a fact, a hint, a name. You spent many intimate hours with her. You may have to spend hours with me. She told you of places she went and people she knew. Tell me."

A muscle on Ballou's neck was twitching. "I insist, I *insist*, that my wife is not to be disturbed. You expect to be paid, naturally. I never 'thrash about.' How much?"

Wolfe nodded. "Naturally for you. Men with money always assume there is no other medium of exchange. I am engaged on behalf of Mr. Cather, and you can't hire me or pay me. I am coercing you, certainly, but only to get information. We shall disturb your wife only if it is requisite. From you I want all the facts, all—"

The phone rang. I turned and got it. "Nero Wolfe's—"

"Saul, Archie. I'm—"

"Hold it," I put it down and moved, to the hall and on to the kitchen, and took the phone.

"We have company. Okay, shoot."

"You're going to have more company. I'm licked. I have met my match. Julie Jaquette. I would give a week's pay to know if you could have handled her. The trouble is partly that Nero Wolfe's a celebrity, so she says, but mostly it's the orchids. If he will show her his orchids she'll tell him all about Isabel Kerr. She won't tell me a damn thing. Nothing."

"Well, well. It might have taken me a whole ten minutes."

"Go soak it. I said a week's pay. She—"

"Where are you?"

"A booth on Christopher Street. The one at the Ten Little Indians had a line waiting. She's working. She'll be off until eight and then from nine-ten to ten-fifteen."

"Then it's simple. Bring her at nine-ten."

"Like hell it's simple." It clicked and he was gone.

I don't expect you to believe me when I report the first words I heard as I re-entered the office, but you have a right to know why we got about as little from Avery Ballou as Saul had got from Julie Jaquette. The words, uttered by Ballou, were, "Rudyard Kipling." As I crossed to my desk my head kept turning to have my eyes on him. As I sat, Wolfe asked him, "The poems?"

"Mostly the poems," Ballou said, "but some of the stories too. And Robert Service and Jack London. A little of some others, but of those three, Kipling and Service and London, I had complete sets there, bound in leather. There's something I have wanted to ask about, but haven't, and you would know. Can they get my fingerprints from those bindings? The leather isn't smooth, it's rippled."

Wolfe's head turned. "Archie?"

"Probably not," I told Ballou, "from rippled leather, but your prints must be on other surfaces there. Are they on file anywhere?"

"I don't know. I simply don't know."

Wolfe's shoulders went up a quarter of an inch and down. "Then on that you can only abide. But this isn't easy to believe, Mr. Ballou, that you spent ten hours or more a week there, five hundred hours a year for three years, and Miss Kerr never spoke of how she spent the other—let's see—nearly twenty-five thousand hours. The places she went, the people she saw."

"I have told you," Ballou said, "under coercion. Except for physical intimacy there was no sharing of experience. But I did not read those poems and stories just to hear myself. I did not impose them on her. She understood them and enjoyed them, and we discussed them. You realize that I am *not* enjoying this. This is the first time in my life that I have wanted to tell a man to go to hell and can't."

"I still find it hard to believe. Did she never speak of her sister?"

"Yes. Speak of her, yes, but casually and rarely."

"You didn't know that her sister strongly disapproved of her association with you?"

"No. I don't know it now."

"She did and does. Did Miss Kerr never mention this name: Julie Jaquette?"

"I don't think so. If she did it was only casual and I don't remember it."

"Remarkable. You were with her, close, frequently, for a period of three years. I wanted and expected names, and you have supplied three: Jack London, Robert Service, and Rudyard Kipling." Wolfe pushed his chair back. "A question: why did you want to know when Mr. Cather first learned your name?"

"Oh . . . I was curious."

"You said it may not be important now. When would it have been important, and why?"

"I meant important to me, not to you, not for what you are trying to do. What *are* you going to do? You say I can't hire you or pay you, but why not? There's no conflict between Cather's interest and mine, as you tell it. Ten thousand now as a retainer? Twenty thousand?"

"No." Wolfe rose. "I'm committed." He walked out.

8

At a quarter past nine we were back in the office and Fritz had taken the coffee things out; so, though I didn't know it yet, the stage was set for one of the most impressive floor shows the old brownstone has ever seen. After letting Ballou out I had gone to the kitchen and told Wolfe about Saul's phone call. Of course he would have enjoyed the onion soup and Kentucky burgoo more if I had waited, but it would have created an atmosphere if I had sprung it on him with the coffee. The question was which could stand it best, appetite or digestion, and it takes a lot to make a serious dent in his appetite.

It is true that digestion was getting it too. He had drunk more coffee than usual, emptying the pot, and now that it was gone, and I was there—I'm usually out on Tuesday evenings—he was making a stab at continuing the dinner conversation, which had been mostly about Viet Nam, but just then he wasn't really interested in Viet Nam. He was going to tackle not only a woman, which was bad enough, but also a nightclub singer, which was preposterous. A hell of a way to spend an evening. When the doorbell rang he glared at me, though he should have saved it for Saul, and I told him so as I got up to go.

Even through the one-way glass, as I approached the door, she took the eye. She was two inches taller than Saul, and if the coat was real sable it must have taken at least a hundred sables. As she entered she gave me a dazzling three-inch smile, and another one when I turned after hanging her coat up. Saul was trying not to grin. She took my arm and asked, "Where is he, Archie?" in a rich cuddly voice, and she kept the arm down the hall and into the office, but then she broke away, danced to the middle of the room and faced Wolfe's desk, let her handbag fall to the floor, and burst into song:

> "Big man, go-go,
> Big man, go big,
> Talk big, act big,
> Lo-o-o-o-o-o-ove big!
> Go-go-go-go-go-go,
> Big man, big man,
> Be big, do big,
> Lo-o-o-o-o-o-ove big,
> Go!"

She extended two long, bare, well-shaped arms to him and said, "Now the orchids. Show me!"

It *was* impressive. So, I admit, was Wolfe. He was giving her exactly the same scowl I have often seen him give a crossword puzzle that had him stumped. He switched the scowl to me and demanded, "Did you suggest this?"

"No," she said. "Nobody ever suggests anything to me; they don't have to. Now the orchids, big man. Go!"

"Miss Jackson," he said.

"Not here," she said. "I'm Julie Jaquette."

"Not here," he said. "It's conceivable that long ago, in different circumstances, I might have appreciated your performance, but not here and—"

"It's not a performance, man, it's me."

"I don't believe it. The creature who pranced in here and mouthed that doggerel couldn't possibly eat or sleep or read or write—or love. Are you capable of love?"

"Ha! Am I!"

Wolfe nodded. "You see? One minute ago you would have said, 'Am I, man.' We're making progress. As for your wish to see my orchids, that can easily be gratified. Either Mr. Panzer or Mr. Goodwin can take you to them at a suitable hour, perhaps tomorrow. Now we have other business, and little time. Do you want the man who killed Isabel Kerr to be exposed and punished?"

"Yes, damn him, I do. I do, man."

Wolfe made a face. "Don't revert. I too want him exposed, because that's the only feasible way to get a man who is in custody released. Orrie Cather. Miss Kerr may have told you of him."

She stared down at him from her five feet nine. "Are you sick?" she demanded.

"No. I am sour, but I'm not sick. If you think Mr. Cather killed her, you're wrong, he didn't, and I'm going to find out who did. Did you?"

Saul and I were standing between her and the door. She turned to us and said distinctly, "You rat."

"Not guilty," Saul said. "You made it plain right away that you thought he killed her. You also made it plain—"

"You said Nero Wolfe wanted me to help nail him."

"I did not. I merely said he wanted you to help. You also made it plain that you would tell me nothing."

She glanced around, went to my chair at my desk, sat, and eyed Wolfe. It would have been quite a lifting job for both of us, so I went to the red leather chair and Saul moved up one of the yellow ones.

"So you think you're going to bounce him," she said. "Because he works for you. Nuts. Tell me how."

Wolfe shook his head. "I can't. I don't know. Manifestly you are satisfied that he's guilty, and of course you have told the police why, but it hasn't fully satisfied them. He is being held only as a material witness. If you care to, try to satisfy me. Why are you so sure?"

"Damn it, I warned her," she said.

"You warned her that Mr. Cather would kill her?"

"No, but I warned her there was no telling *what* he would do. I suppose you know he wanted to marry another girl?"

"Yes."

"So it was an ungodly mess, the kind people get into when a screw gets loose. They had a perfect setup, the damn fools. Whoever was paying her bills, she never told me who it was, he had a place with her in it whenever he needed a change, and you couldn't beat that. She had the place to herself most of the time, and she had a man who did her good, and you couln't beat *that*. He had a woman who suited him, ready for him nearly any time, for nothing, and you couldn't beat *that*. A perfect setup. But she decides she has got to marry him, and he decides he has got to marry some other dame, and even *she* has got a good job—an airline stewardess. You know that?"

"Yes."

"So she could stay loose too if she had any brains. None of them had any brains. I warned Isabel she had better deal him out, he had the sweat up and might do anything, but she wouldn't listen. She put the sting on him, and he killed her. When people's brains quit working, just go somewhere else. But he killed her, and now he'll have to go somewhere else."

"You have told the police all this?"

"I sure have."

"What if he didn't kill her?"

"Nuts."

Wolfe regarded her. Since his eyes were used to seeing me when they aimed at that chair, he had to adjust. "Do you ever gamble?" he asked her. "Do you like to bet?"

"That's a silly question. Who doesn't?"

"Good. Saul, what odds will you give Miss Jackson that Orrie Cather didn't kill Isabel Kerr?"

Saul didn't hesitate. "Ten to one." He got his wallet from a pocket and took bills out. "A hundred to ten."

"She may not have it. Will you—"

"I always have it." She opened her bag, which she had put on my desk after picking it up from the floor, where she had dropped it while performing. "But who settles it?"

"The District Attorney," Saul said. "A hundred to ten that he isn't even tried. All right for Archie Goodwin to hold it?"

"No. Nero Wolfe." She got up and handed Wolfe a bill, and Saul went with his. Wolfe checked Saul's, five twenties, opened a drawer, and dropped them in. She went back to my chair, put her bag on my desk, and told Wolfe, "Now tell me why I have just lost ten bucks."

He shook his head. "That must await the event. I merely wished to demonstrate that we are acting on a conclusion, not a conjecture. Do you have animus for Mr. Cather?"

"What's animus?"

"Hostility. Hatred."

"Of course not. I don't hate anybody."

"If he didn't kill Miss Kerr, you are willing to lose that ten dollars?"

"Why not? It's a bet."

"Then if someone else killed her you would rather have him justly punished than Mr. Cather wrongfully punished?"

"Certainly."

"Again, good. You and Miss Kerr were close friends. Except for the name of the man who was paying her bills, she confided in you. What kind of woman was she? That question is not at random; I need to know. What was she like?"

"She was a duck. She was a damn fine woman until she flapped about that square. She knew the game and she knew the score. She always had her dignity, all the way. She had a good big heart, but she never let it *bleed*. I'd rather not have any heart than have it bleeding around everywhere. One reason we were so close was that we both knew exactly what men are for and what they're not for—until that Cather baboon popped up."

"You know him?"

"No. I've never seen him and I don't want to."

Wolfe looked at the clock. "You must be back at a quarter past ten?"

"At ten past ten. I have to change."

"Then we haven't much time. I ask you to accept a hypothesis. Suppose you knew positively, no matter how, that he did *not* kill her. Then who did? Whom would you suspect?"

"That's easy. The lobster, of course."

"What? Lobster?"

"Excuse me. The man who was keeping her."

"You don't even know his name."

"So what? He was shelling out around twenty grand a year. Maybe it was stripping him. Maybe he was hooking it. He found out about that Cather, and he killed her. That's ABC."

"Very well, I'll consider it. But extend the hypothesis. Eliminate him too. Who then? Didn't you and Miss Kerr have many mutual friends?"

"Yes. If you want to call them friends to be polite. Sure we did."

"Suppose it was one of them. Which one?"

She pronounced a word which she should have kept to herself, since there was a lady present.

"Meaning?" Wolfe asked.

"Meaning I know them. You don't kill someone unless you have a reason, and even if you have a reason you've got to have the guts. They don't fit."

"Not one?"

"No."

"Will you give Mr. Goodwin or Mr. Panzer some of their names while he is showing you the orchids?"

"He can't show me the orchids. I have to be going."

"Perhaps tomorrow morning."

He'd have to bring them to me in bed. Spread them all over me. I'd like that, but he wouldn't. In bed in the morning I'm no treat."

"Then the afternoon. Have you ever met a Dr. Gamm?"

"Teddy?" She laughed. "Yes, I know Teddy. I guess he's a pretty good doctor, but as a man you can have him. He got the idea he was going to make Isabel, and that *was* an idea. God knows what he'll do for an idea now."

"That one didn't work?"

"Certainly not."

"Have you ever met Miss Kerr's sister? Mrs. Fleming?"

She nodded. "*That* beetle. Now there's an idea. It's not funny, either. I honestly believe she thought Isabel would be better off dead. All right, if it wasn't Cather and it wasn't the lobster, it was her." She looked at the wall clock. "I've got to go." She left my chair. "Come along. Why not? You can have a front table aand I'll spot you. I'll announce you big. I'll tell the suckers that Nero Wolfe in person is here and will take a bow. You can bow sitting down if you want to, they'll stand on their chairs to see you. It will be a feather in my bra. Come along. The beer will be on the house."

Wolfe's head was tilted back to squint up at her. "I decline your invitation, Miss Jackson," he said, "but I wish you well. I have the impression that your opinion of our fellow beings and their qualities is somewhat similar to mine." He got to his feet. He almost never stands for comers or goers, male or female. And he actually repeated it. "I wish you well, madam."

"Big man," she said. She turned. "You come, Archie. That Panzer's a rat."

9

Forty-seven hours later, at nine o'clock Thursday evening, Wolfe put his coffee cup down and said, "Four days and nights of nothingness."

I put my cup down and said, "No argument."

Actually there could have been one. There had been plenty of nothingness in results, but not in efforts. Somewhere in the nine notebooks here on my table— I write these reports on my own machine up in my room, not in the office—are the names of four males and six females, supplied by Jaquette-Jackson when she came to look at the orchids Wednesday afternoon, who had been seen by Saul and Fred. For something to bite on, hopeless. Of course anything is possible. It was possible that one of the women had thought that Isabel had pinched her lipstick and had gone to get it and got mad and bopped her, or that one of the men hated Rudyard Kipling and couldn't stand a woman who had him bound in leather, but you need something better than ten billion possibles to get your teeth into. Any little piece of straw will do, but you have to have *something*.

For instance, statistics. There are two kinds of statistics, the kind you look up and the kind you make up. I admit this is the second kind: out of every thousand murders committed by amateurs, eighty-three are a woman killing another woman because she has taken her husband, or part of him. Therefore, from the statistical point of view, on the list of names we had collected the only one with a worthy known motive was Mrs. Avery Ballou, and that automatically gave her top billing. The difficulty was the approach. If I went and asked her if she had known that her husband had for three years been reading Kipling's poems to the woman who had been murdered last week, Ballou would never speak to us again, and we might need him for something. So after breakfast Wednesday morning I rang Lily Rowan and asked her if she had ever met Mrs. Avery Ballou, and she said no, and from the little she knew about her she didn't particularly care to.

"Then I won't insist," I said. "But I need to find out if I want to meet her. This is strictly private. I don't need a detailed résumé, just a sketch, especially what her main interests are. For instance, if she collects autographs of famous private detectives, that would be perfect."

"She *can't* be *that* sappy."

I said she might do worse and it was a rush order, and an hour later she called me back. She had more than I needed, and I'll omit most of it. Mrs. Ballou had been Minerva Chadwick of the steel and railroad Chadwicks. She had married Ballou in 1936. Their son and two daughters were married. Her friends called her Minna. She never gave big parties but liked to have a few friends in for dinner. She was an Episcopalian but seldom went to church. She didn't like Paris much and she hated Florida. She liked horses and had four Arabians, but her special interest was Irish wolfhounds, and she had either twelve or fourteen. . . .

I have wasted my space and your time, since obviously it was Irish wolfhounds. About all I knew about them was that they are big, so I called a man I know who knows dogs and got a few facts, and then rang the listed number of the Ballou house on 67th Street. When a voice like a butler said, "Mrs.

Ballou's residence," I told him my name was Archibald Goodwin and I would like to make an appointment with Mrs. Ballou to ask her advice about an Irish wolfhound. He said she was not then available and he would give her the message, and I gave him my phone number. Toward noon a call came, a businesslike female voice who said she was Miss Corcoran, Mrs. Ballou's secretary, and what kind of advice did I want about an Irish wolfhound. I told her I was thinking of buying one, and I didn't know which of the commercial kennels had the best ones, and a friend had told me that Mrs. Ballou knew more about it than anyone else in the country; and she said if I came at five o'clock Mrs. Ballou would see me. That was okay, since Jackson-Jaquette was due at two-thirty to look at orchids.

You probably have no strong desire to spend another couple of hours with either Julie Jaquette or Miss Jackson, and I have already reported on the ten names I got from her, so I'll skip it and give you the pleasure of meeting Minna Ballou. The setting and supporting cast were fully up to expectations: the butler who let me in, with keen, careful eyes that sized me up in two seconds; the mat that protected the first six feet of the rug in the reception hall, bigger than the 14-by-26 Keraghan in Wolfe's office; the uniformed maid who turned her nose up as she took my hat and coat; the wide marble stairs; the elevator with red lacquered panels; the middle-aged gray-haired gray-eyed Miss Corcoran, who was there when I stepped out on the fourth floor; the room she took me to, with a desk and typewriter and cabinets to the left, and a couch and soft chairs and a coffee table to the right. Pictures of dogs and horses were spotted around, but my glance caught no picture of Avery Ballou. His wife was stretched out on the couch, on her back, with what I would call a faded red bathrobe reaching down nearly to her ankles. As we entered she turned her

head and said, "I hoped you wouldn't come. I'm tired."
She pointed to a chair near the foot of the couch.
"Sit there."

I obeyed the order and was facing her. She had
thin lips and a thin nose, and a twist of her dyed
brown hair straggled down her forehead. She was
barefooted and her toes bulged. I smiled at her
cordially.

"Aren't you going to say anything?" she demanded.

"If you're not too tired," I said, "I suppose Miss
Corcoran told you what I said on the phone. Actually
it's a friend of mine who wants to get an Irish wolfhound. She has a place up in Westchester. I live in
town, and I guess a city apartment is no place for
an Irish wolfhound."

"It certainly isn't."

"Somebody told her she should get one from Ireland."

"Who told her that?"

"I don't know."

"Whoever it was, he's a fool. Commercial breeders
in Ireland have very inferior stock. The best wolfhound breeder in the world is Florence Nagle in
England, but she's not commercial, and she's very
particular whom she sells to. All good breeders are. Of
course I'm not commercial either, I sell only as a very
special favor. I love wolfhounds and they love me.
When I'm there, eight of them sleep in my bedroom."

I smiled nicely. "Does your husband like that?"

"I doubt if he even knows it. He wouldn't know a
wolfhound from a ostrich. What's your friend's name?"

"Lily Rowan. Her place is near Katonah."

"Why does she want a wolfhound?"

"Well, partly for protection. There are no close
neighbors."

"That reason's not good enough. You have to love
them. You have to like it when a tail knocks over a
vase or a lamp. Does she know that a good male
weighs up to a hundred and thirty pounds, and when
he rears up he's six feet six? Does she know that

when he leaps at you because he loves you, you go down? Does she know that he has to run three miles a day and you have to tailgate him behind a station wagon? Tell her to get just a dog, a Great Dane or a Doberman."

I shook my head. "I don't think that's very smart, Mrs. Ballou."

"I do. Why not?"

"Because you ought to realize that Miss Rowan is all set to love an Irish wolfhound. Look at the trouble she's taking. She finds out about kennels, but that doesn't satisfy her, and she hears that the person who knows most about it is you, and she gets me to try to see you, because she thinks a man would stand a better chance with you than another woman. I told her she could do it herself by seeing your husband, but she didn't know if he was interested in wolfhounds. Apparently he isn't."

She closed her eyes and opened them again. "My husband is interested in absolutely nothing but finance and what he calls the structure of economics. What's the name of that Englishwoman who writes books about it?"

"Barbara Ward."

She nodded. "She might interest him, but no other woman would. What's your friend's name?"

"Lily Rowan."

"Yes. I'm tired. You seem to have some sense. Do *you* think a wolfhound would be happy with her?"

"I do, or I wouldn't be here."

"Does she want a male or a bitch?"

"I was told to ask you. Which would you advise?"

"It depends. I would have to know . . . she lives in the country?"

"Not in the winter. She has an apartment in town." I didn't add that her penthouse was about four hundred yards from where I was sitting.

"I would have to see her." She turned her head. "Celia, have you got that name? Lucy Rowan?"

Miss Corcoran, at the desk, said yes, she had it, and

Mrs. Ballou returned to me. "Tell her to call Miss Corcoran. That's what she should have done instead of bothering you. I didn't get your name . . . it doesn't matter." She shut her eyes.

I arose and stood, thinking it would be better manners to thank her with her eyes open, but they didn't open, so I said thank you, and she said with her eyes shut, "I thought you had gone." If I had been an Irish wolfhound I would have wagged my tail as I left the room and knocked something over. Miss Corcoran, who accompanied me to the elevator to see that I entered it, told me that between ten and eleven in the morning would be the best time for Miss Rowan to phone.

I hadn't had a decent walk since Saturday, it wasn't five-thirty yet, and I might as well save taxi fare. But first there was a phone call to make, so I went to Madison Avenue, found a booth, got Lily Rowan, explained the situation, and said that she had better ring Miss Corcoran in the morning and tell her she had decided to get a dachshund instead. What she said was irrelevant and personal. Outside again, I turned my collar up and put gloves on. Winter was going all out.

If you have the impression that the help was doing all the work, Saul and Fred after the ten names I had got from Julie Jaquette and me cornering a jealous wife, no indeed. When I entered the office at a quarter past six there was Wolfe at his desk with a book, and I saw at a glance that it wasn't *Invitation to an Inquest*. It was *The Jungle Book* by Rudyard Kipling, so I tiptoed across to my desk, not to disturb him. When he finished a paragraph and looked up I asked, "Wouldn't you get the feel better if you read aloud? Pretend I'm her."

He ignored it and demanded, "Have you done any better?"

"No, sir. Unless we want an Irish wolfhound for stalking. Mrs. Ballou is scratched. Even if someone had told her all about it, full details, she couldn't have gone there and settled Isabel Kerr because (a) she would have been too tired, and (b) she would have forgotten the name and address. Of course Miss Jackson has broadened your understanding of women, and you may not agree."

I reported. It was so brief that he hadn't much more than got comfortably arranged, leaning back with his eyes closed, when I reached the end, the phone call to Lily Rowan.

"There is one difference between you and her," I said. "You shut your eyes to concentrate on what I'm saying, and she shuts hers to hope I'm not there. She didn't even notice that I dragged her husband in by the heels, twice. I swear I could have told her all about Isabel Kerr and the pink bedroom, and when he came home from work she wouldn't have bothered to mention it to him."

He grunted and opened his eyes. "How could eight dogs that size possibly spend the night in her bedroom?" he demanded.

I nodded. "That worried me too. If you figure an average of two square yards to a dog, and maybe more if—"

The doorbell rang, and I went. It was a man in a heavy brown tweed overcoat and a smooth dark blue narrow-rimmed hat, which was ridiculous, and I guessed it was one of the bozos Saul or Fred had flushed. But when I opened the door he said, "I am Dr. Gamm. Theodore Gamm, M.D. Are you the man who called on Mr. and Mrs. Fleming Monday afternoon?" I told him yes, and he said, "I insist on seeing Nero Wolfe," and would have walked right through me if I hadn't sidestepped.

Of course that isn't the way to do it. You merely say something first and *then* you insist. He wasn't even built for it, after he peeled his coat off. He was round all over, round-shouldered and round-hipped and round-faced, and the bald top of his head was barely up to my chin. I put him in the front room, took the long route to the office, by the hall, and told Wolfe that Dr. Theodore Gamm insisted on asking him why he had sent me to see Mr. and Mrs. Fleming. He looked at the clock and growled, "Dinner in half an hour." I said that Mrs. Ballou had taken me only ten minutes, went and opened the connecting door, and brought him in. As I motioned him to the red leather chair Wolfe said something about twenty minutes. That chair is deep, and when he found that his feet weren't on the floor he slid forward, pinned his eyes on Wolfe, and said, "You're grossly overweight."

Wolfe nodded. "Seventy pounds. Perhaps eighty. Death will see to that. Does it concern you?"

"Yes, it does." He curled his pudgy hands over the ends of the chair arms. "Any conflict with natural health is an impertinence, and I resent it." His voice was bigger than he was. "It is my concern for health that brought me here—the health of one of my patients, Mrs. Barry Fleming. You sent a man—that man—" his eyes darted to me and back to Wolfe— "to torment her. She was already in a state of strain, and now she threatens to collapse. Can you justify it?"

"Easily." Wolfe's brows were up. "Both the intention and the deed, but it's the deed you challenge. Mrs. Fleming's state of strain was partly from the shock of her sister's death, but mostly from the fear that her way of life would be exposed. Mr. Goodwin rendered her a service by making it clear that the exposure is inevitable unless certain steps are taken. That should propel her not to collapse, but to action, if she is—"

"What kind of action?"

"The only kind that could be effective. Did she tell you all that Mr. Goodwin said?"

"Her husband did. That if the man they have arrested, Orrie Cather, is tried, everything about Isabel will come out. That Cather is innocent, and the only hope is to get enough evidence to make them release him. You call that a service, to tell her that?"

"If it's valid, yes. It's obvious. Do you question it?"

"Yes. I think it was a cheap trick. Why do you say Cather is innocent? Can you prove it?"

"No, but I intend to."

"I don't believe it. I think you're merely trying to raise enough dust to make it hard to convict him. There is no reason why you should want to do Mrs. Fleming a service, but if you did want to you could. You could persuade Cather and his lawyer to make it unnecessary for certain facts to be brought out at his trial. I know you won't, but you could."

"You would like me to?"

"Certainly. For Mrs. Fleming that—it might save her life."

"But you know I won't?"

"Yes."

"Then why did you bother to come?"

"She asked me to. They both did. They think it was just a trick, your sending him with that hogwash, and so do I. Why do you say Cather is innocent?"

Wolfe squinted at him. "You should arrange your mind better, Doctor. As Mr. Goodwin explained to Mrs. Fleming, it will serve her interest if Mr. Cather is innocent, but you don't like that. You contend. Is it possible that you are less concerned about your patient's health than about your own? Did you kill Isabel Kerr?"

Gamm goggled. "Why, you—" He swallowed. "Damn your impertinence!"

"Naturally you damn it. But since I have assumed that Mr. Cather did not kill her, for reasons I prefer not to disclose, I need to know who did. As a man whose repeated advances to her were spurned, you are eligible. Persistent mortification can become insupportable. It's a question of character and temperament, and I know nothing of yours; I would have to consult people who know you well—for instance, Mr. and Mrs. Fleming. But I can collect facts. Where were you last Saturday morning from eight o'clock to noon? If you can establish—"

He stopped because his audience was going. Dr.

Gamm didn't have the figure or the style for an impressive exit, it was more like a waddle, but it got him to the door and on through. I took my time rising and crossing to the hall, and got there just as he was opening the front door. When he was out and the door closed I went back in, raised my arms for a good stretch and an uncovered yawn, and said, "Another one down. He wouldn't have walked out, he wouldn't have dared, until he found out if you have anything and how much. Or tried to."

Wolfe's lips were tight. He loosened them to say, "He's either a murderer or a jackass."

"Then he's a jackass. It seems to me—"

The phone rang and I went and got it. It was Saul, reporting on a couple of names. I told him we could match him and wished him better luck tomorrow.

He didn't have it, and neither did we. Thursday was even emptier than Wednesday, though I tried hard because Wolfe had paid me a compliment. Partly he was merely desperate, but the fact remains that Wednesday evening he told me to go and give the neighborhood a play. It was the first time he had ever sent me on something that Saul had already covered, and I admit it would have been highly satisfactory to get a break—for example, a janitor across the street who had seen a stranger enter that building Saturday morning, a stranger who could have been Dr. Gamm or Stella Fleming or Barry Fleming or Julie Jaquette, or even Avery or Minna Ballou. Or even just a stranger, to try to find. What the hell, there are only twelve million people in the metropolitan area. Actually it was a farce without a laugh. Not only had Saul and Fred seen everyone, but also the cops had worked it hard, trying to find somebody who could put Orrie Cather there. During the long day I spoke with more than forty people, all ages and sizes and colors, and they had already been spoken to so often that they had their answers down pat. At six-thirty I called it a week and went home to dinner. The only thing that had happened there was that Parker had called to say that he had seen Orrie again, and had talked with an assistant district attorney, and he still thought it was inadvisable to start action to get him out on bail.

So back in the office after dinner Wolfe put his coffee cup down and said, "Four days and nights of nothingness," and I put mine down and said, "No argument."

"Confound it," Wolfe said, "ask questions."

"If there were any good ones," I said, "you would ask them yourself. All right, Jill Hardy. Why did she want my arms around her? Because she had killed Isabel Kerr and was going to confess and wanted to soften me up but Cramer interrupted?"

"I don't want chaff. I want a question."

"So do I. Stella Fleming. She is subject to fits, for instance going for me with claws. But if she had one Saturday morning and killed her sister, would she have gone back that evening and got the superintendent to let her in so she could discover the body? I don't believe it. A thousand to one."

"Negative," he muttered. "Something positive."

"Try this. Barry Fleming. Why did he invite me in, knowing how his wife was? Because I had told him we were going to clear Orrie, and he wanted to find out if we knew or suspected that *he* had killed Isabel. That's positive."

"But vain without a motive."

"Oh, if you want motive. Mrs. Ballou. Her chat with me was a production. She's really a hellcat and nuts about her husband. Boiling with jealousy. Only in that case I'm a sap and you'll have to fire me."

"I'll consider it. Mr. Ballou."

I shook my head. "Your turn. You had him."

"I reject him, provisionally. Cracking that woman's skull with an ashtray was an act of passion, not within his compass. There is a question: why would he like to know when Orrie first heard his name? Why is it not important now but still he would like to know?"

I shook my head again. "We'd better skip that. Probably curiosity as to whether it coincided with a change he noticed in the way she reacted to Kipling and Service and London. That wouldn't interest you. I agree on his compass. All right, Miss Jackson. She's yours too, you wished her well."

"No. Yours."

"Thank you. There is nothing she couldn't and wouldn't do if it appealed to her. But if she had any reason for wanting Isabel dead I would have to see it in color, with sound. Talking with ten of their mutual friends, Saul or Fred would surely have got a hint, especially Saul. And they didn't. Anyway she's crossed off since you wished her well. So we're down to Dr. Gamm."

"Pfui."

"I agree. We're down to nothing. You told us Sunday evening that we have never had less, and you can say it again. Not a sign of a crack anywhere. I was thinking during dinner, while you were commenting on what they intend to do to Ellis Island, that maybe you should make a deal with Cramer. I mean it. His scientists didn't miss an inch of that apartment, and there's a chance that whoever killed her left his prints somewhere, at least one. They latched onto Orrie so fast that they have probably filed other possibilities. Offer to trade Cramer all we have for all the prints they got. With your word of honor, which he knows is good. It wouldn't sink Orrie any deeper, and it just might give us a lead. As it stands, there isn't one single damn item on the program for tomorrow."

His jaw was set. "No," he said.

"No what? If you prefer—"

The doorbell rang. I went, took a look, stuck my head back in, and said, "Mr. Ballou. He doesn't look jaunty."

10

If Avery Ballou had somehow dropped all his stack, and had been kicked out of his job as president of the Federal Holding Corporation, he wouldn't have starved. I have never seen a neater job of wrapping and taping than he had done on the little package he put on Wolfe's desk before he sat down. Any shipping room in town would have grabbed him. I am assuming that he had done it himself on account of what was in it, but I admit it might have been packaged at the bank. The seams in his face were deeper than ever, and he looked as tired as his wife had felt. Seated, he lowered his head and rubbed his brow with a palm, slowly back and forth. On Tuesday that had been followed by a request for a drink, but now apparently he was beyond that. He raised his head, pulled his shoulders up, looked at Wolfe, and said, "You said I couldn't hire you or pay you."

"And told you why," Wolfe said.

"I know. But the situation is—I want you to reconsider it." He turned to me. "You said you could find out when that man Cather learned my name. Have you?"

I shook my head. "You said it isn't important now."

"You also said it could have been as long as four months ago."

"Right. I said 'certainly.' Or eight months, or ten."

"Four is enough." He returned to Wolfe. "I know you have had a wide experience, but you may not realize the absolute necessity of good repute for a man of my standing. Byron wrote 'The glory and the nothing of a name,' but he was a poet. A poet can take liberties that are fatal to a man like me. As I think I told you, I took great precautions when I visited Miss Kerr. No one who ever saw me enter or leave that building could possibly have recognized me. I had full reliance on her discretion; I was more than liberal with her, financially. I was completely certain that nobody whatever knew of my . . . diversion."

He stopped, apparently inviting comment. Wolfe obliged. "You should know that your only safe secrets are those you have yourself forgotten."

He nodded. "I now suspect that there are many things I should know that I don't know. My reliance on Miss Kerr was misplaced. I was a fool. I should have known that she might . . . form an attachment. I assume she did, with Cather? She became attached to him?"

Wolfe turned to me. "Archie?"

"She burned," I told Ballou. "She wanted to marry him."

"I see. I was a fool. But that explains why she told him my name, and that's important. She *was* discreet, but of course with him there was no discretion. Doesn't that follow?"

He wanted an answer, and Wolfe supplied it. "Yes."

"Then he knew my name, but no one else did. Then he's a scoundrel and a blackmailer. I have been paying him a thousand dollars a month for four months. Almost certainly he is also a murderer. He killed her. I don't know why he killed her, but he's a scoundrel."

Wolfe's eyes came to me, and I met them. I put one brow up. His eyes went back to Ballou. "Why the devil," he demanded, "didn't you tell me this before? Two days ago."

"I didn't see it then. Not as I do now, after considering it. You had given me a bad jolt. And you had said that Cather didn't kill her. I think he did.

He's a blackguard. I think he'll be tried and convicted, and that's why I'm here. You said the other day that if he is tried my name will inevitably be divulged, and *that must not happen*. My name connected not merely with a diversion but with a sensational murder—it *must not happen*." He pointed to the package he had put on Wolfe's desk. "That parcel contains fifty thousand dollars in fifty-dollar bills. You told me the other day that you were committed, but you don't have to stay committed to a blackmailer and a murderer."

He took a breath. "That fifty thousand is just a retainer. I'm in a tougher trap than I realized, and I have to get out, no matter what it costs. I admit I don't see how it can be done, but you know Cather and you'll know how to deal with him. I'm not asking or expecting anything crooked. If they have the evidence to try him and convict him, all right, that's the law. But my name *must not appear*. You said that, since no one has called on me, my name isn't in that diary, and also evidently Cather hasn't mentioned my name to the police. Isn't that true?"

"Yes." Wolfe was pinching his lip with a thumbtip and a fingertip. "You're going much too fast, Mr. Ballou. I concede that I don't have to stay committed to a blackmailer and a murderer, but am I? I need to know more. Describe the man you paid the money to."

"I have never seen him. I mailed it to him."

"When and how did he demand it?"

"On the telephone. One evening in September, at my home, I was told that a man who gave his name as Robert Service Kipling wished to speak to me. Of course I took the phone. He told me that he didn't have to explain why he used that name and told me to go to a nearby drugstore and be at the booth at ten o'clock and answer the phone when it rang. You will understand why I went. At ten o'clock the phone rang in the booth, and I answered it. It was the same voice. It isn't necessary to tell you what he said. He said enough to convince me that he knew of my visits to that apartment and their purpose. He said he had no desire to interfere with them, and he thought I should show my appreciation for his cooperation. He told me to mail him ten hundred-dollar bills the next day, and the same amount on the fifteenth of each month. I said I would."

He rubbed his brow with a palm. "I know it is wrong, on principle, to submit to blackmail. But the threat was not exposure, he didn't say he had evidence in his possession, he merely made it plain that I would have to pay him or stop going there. He wouldn't answer my questions, how had he learned my name, but obviously he hadn't merely seen me and recognized me, from things he said. Just his giving his name as Robert Service Kipling would have been enough for that. I mailed the money the next day, and each month since. I simply preferred to pay him rather than give it up. Now I know. Unquestionably it was Cather. Miss Kerr had told him."

Wolfe nodded. "A reasonable conjecture, but that's all. His name and address, for mailing?"

"It was a fake name, naturally. The address was General Delivery, Grand Central Station, Lexington Avenue and Forty-fifth Street. The name was Milton Thales."

"Thales? T,H,A,L,E,S?"

"Yes."

"Indeed. Interesting." Wolfe closed his eyes and in a moment opened them. "You made no effort to learn who he was?"

"No. What for? What good would that do?"

"If it was Mr. Cather, it might have prevented this. Did you tell Miss Kerr about it?"

"Yes. I asked if she had told anyone, *anyone*, my name, and she said she hadn't. She lied. She was very—well, she was indignant. I was a little surprised at her reaction. It didn't seem to be—" He stopped. He pursed his lips and frowned, and then he nodded. "I see. Of course. I said I don't know why he killed her, but it's obvious. She knew it must be Cather, and she told him, and she told him he had to stop, and he killed her. My God, if I had known—damn him. *Damn him!*"

It was closer to passion that I had thought was in his compass, and I was going to offer him a drink, but Wolfe spoke. "A detail. The voice on the telephone. Indubitably a man?"

"Yes. He was disguising it, a kind of falsetto, but I was sure it was a man. No doubt at all."

"Has he communicated with you again? Telephoned?"

"Once. The seventeenth of December. That name again, Robert Service Kipling. At my home. He said he thought I would like to know that the material was being received, and that was all."

Wolfe leaned back, closed his eyes, clasped his hands at the high point of his middle, and pushed his lips out. Ballou started to say something, and I showed him a palm, but it really didn't matter. When Wolfe's lips start working like that, out and in, out and in, he has taken off and he hears nothing. Ballou lowered his head and shut *his* eyes, so in effect I was left alone for about three minutes. Finally Wolfe opened his eyes and asked me if I could get Saul and Fred, and I said yes but I didn't know how soon. He said, "The kitchen. Tell them to come at once," and I went.

Making phone calls merely to tell men they're wanted—I had to try three numbers to get Saul— doesn't take much brainpower, and my mind could work on something else. Not figuring the odds on Orrie as a blackmailer; that was so long a shot it was just no bet. The riddle was, why was Thales an interesting name for a blackmailer? Wolfe had really meant it; it wasn't the tone he uses when he's faking. If he thought it was interesting I should too, since I knew everything he did. I would give a nice new dollar bill to know how many of the people who read this report will be on to it. I still wasn't when I returned to the office, though I sat and pecked at it for a good five minutes after I got Saul.

Two paces inside the office I stopped. The red leather chair was empty. I asked Wolfe, "Did you bounce him?"

He shook his head. "He's in the front room. Lying down. Of course he shouldn't be seen by Saul and Fred. You got them?"

"They're on the way." I crossed to my desk. "It's too bad Orrie sank to blackmail, but then a wedding ring, furniture, marriage license—it mounts up."

"Nonsense."

"You can say that, with fifty grand there on your desk. Why is it interesting that he picked Thales for a name?"

"You mispronounce it. So did Mr. Ballou."

"It isn't Thales?"

"Certainly not. It's Thā-lēz."

"Oh, that's why it's interesting."

"The Milton is interesting too. Thales of Miletus, the sixth and seventh centuries B.C., was the chief of the seven 'wise men' of ancient Greece. He preceded Euclid by three centuries. He founded the geometry of lines. He made the first prediction of an eclipse of the sun, to the day. His was the first great name in the history of mathematics. Thales of Miletus."

"I'll be damned." I sat and looked at it for a full minute. "I *will* be damned. He had a hell of a nerve. Ballou went to college. He might have liked mathematics. He might have known all about Thales of Miletus."

"But did he know that Miss Kerr's brother-in-law is a teacher of mathematics?"

"Probably not. Who would ever expect a goddam blackmailer to have a sense of humor? Did you tell Ballou?"

"No. It can wait. I would like some beer."

"And I would like some milk." I rose. "This is more like it, something to chew on." I went to the kitchen. Fritz was below in his room, and I didn't need any help. As I poured the milk and put the beer and glass on the tray, and took them to the office, my mind was on the newer and hotter riddle, going back to Monday afternoon and remembering how Barry Fleming had looked and acted and what he had said. After a couple of sips of milk, recollecting that we had a guest, I went to the front room to ask if he would like a drink. He was stretched out on the sofa with his arm curled over his eyes. He didn't want anything. In the short time I was gone Wolfe had been to the shelves and got a book, a volume of the Britannica, and had it open. As I picked up my glass he said, "Thales perfected the theory of the scalene triangle and the theory of lines. He discovered the theorem that the sides of equiangular triangles are proportional. He discovered that when two straight lines intersect the vertically opposite angles are equal, and that the circle is bisected by its diameter."

I said, "Golly."

It was close to eleven o'clock when Fred arrived. I took him to the kitchen, because Wolfe was still consulting the encyclopedia, though he must have finished with Thales long ago. When Saul came, I sent him to join Fred in the kitchen and told Wolfe to let us know when he was ready for company, and he glared at me because he was in the middle of an interesting article. The way I know it was interesting is that there isn't a single page in the whole twenty-four volumes that he wouldn't think was interesting. I went to the kitchen and brought them, and Saul took the red leather chair and Fred one of the yellow ones.

That was the shortest session with the help on record. "I apologize," Wolfe said, "for getting you out so late on a winter night, but I need you. There has been a development. The man who maintained that apartment for Miss Kerr—call him X—is in the front room. He came to tell me something that he should have told me two days ago. Last September a man telephoned him and demanded money. The man knew of his visits to that apartment and threatened to make them impossible unless the money was paid, a thousand dollars at once and a thousand dollars a month, in cash, to be mailed to him at general delivery—an assumed name, of course. The money has been paid, a total of five thousand dollars. X is convinced, for reasons he considers valid, that the blackmailer is Orrie Cather. Sunday evening I asked your opinion as to whether Orrie had killed Miss Kerr. I now ask your opinion as to whether he is a blackmailer. Did he blackmail X? Fred?"

Fred was frowning, concentrating. "Just like you said?" he asked. "Just straight open-and-shut blackmail?"

"Yes."

Fred shook his head. "No, sir. Impossible."

"Saul?"

"To be sure I have it right," Saul said, "this was at the time when Orrie was seeing her himself?"

"Yes."

"Then no. As Fred said, impossible. That would take a real snake."

"Satisfactory," Wolfe said. "Archie and I had made our conclusion, and I know, barely short of certainty, who the blackmailer is, but I wanted your opinions. I didn't get you here just for that; there will be instructions for tomorrow. Archie, may they wait in your room?"

Not the kitchen. He was taking no chances. What if a man-eating tiger bounded in through the kitchen window and they scooted down the hall and saw Ballou? I told them they were welcome to my room as long as they didn't rummage, and they headed for the stairs. Wolfe gave them a full minute to get up the two flights and then told me to bring Ballou. He was still on the sofa, but when I entered he sat up and started talking. I told him to save it for Wolfe, and he got to his feet and came. I swear his first glance, as he crossed to the red leather chair, was at the package on Wolfe's desk. A habit is a habit, even when you're up a tree.

As he sat, he spoke. "I've been going over it. I have answered your questions, and I have made you a liberal offer, more than liberal. Either you accept it or you don't. The other day you told me Cather wasn't a murderer. Don't try to tell me now that he's not a blackmailer."

"You anticipate me," Wolfe said. "Mr. Cather is not a blackmailer."

Ballou stared. "You actually—after what I . . ." He rose and picked up the package. "By God, you *are* committed."

"I am indeed. I can name the blackmailer. Sit down."

"I have already named him."

"No. You know only his *noms de guerre*, Robert Service Kipling and Milton Thales. His real name is Barry Fleming. The husband of Miss Kerr's sister."

"That's absurd. You didn't even know I had been blackmailed until an hour ago."

Wolfe would have had to slant his head back to focus on his face, and he doesn't like to, so he wasn't focusing at all. "For a man of affairs," he said, "you're remarkably obtuse. You're in a pickle, and I am your only hope. You must have help, and you can't go to a lawyer, or to anyone, without disclosing your connection with Miss Kerr and a murder. But you talk and act as if you were in control. You spring to your feet and grab that package of money. Pfui. You probably have no further information for me. Either sit down and listen, or go."

You have to hand it to the president of the Federal Holding Corporation. He had pride and he had grit. If he had put the package back on Wolfe's desk he would have been buckling under, so he didn't. He put it on the little stand by the red leather chair, and there it was at his elbow when he sat, under his control.

"I'm listening," he said.

"That's better," Wolfe said. "First, Mr. Cather. Knowledge of a man cannot alone exclude him as a murderer, but it can as a blackmailer. Murder can be merely a spasm, but not blackmail. Four of us who have known Mr. Cather well for years—the two men I sent for, and Mr. Goodwin and I—agree that it can't possibly be Mr. Cather who blackmailed you. Now, the blackmailer. That name, Milton Thales—pronouncing it as you did and as almost any American would. But if I pronounce it Thā-lēz does it stir your memory?"

"Should it?"

"Yes."

He was frowning. "Thā-lēz—why, yes. An early Greek . . . eclipse of the sun . . . geometry . . ."

Wolfe nodded. "That's enough. A renowned name in the history of mathematics. Thā-lēz of Miletus. Milton Thales. Barry Fleming, Miss Kerr's brother-in-law, teaches mathematics at a high school. Miss Kerr told her sister your name, and she told her husband. So I have named the blackmailer."

"Thā-lēz," Ballou said. "Thales. Miletus. Milton. By God, I believe you have. And Isabel—Miss Kerr told me she had told my name to no one. She lied. I wonder how many more."

"Probably none. Those two were special to her. I think we may assume that only five people know of your connection with Miss Kerr: Mr. Cather, Mr. and Mrs. Fleming, Mr. Goodwin, and I. And only three know you were blackmailed, besides the blackmailer: Mr. Goodwin, you, and I. The two men upstairs, out of hearing, know of the blackmail, but not of you. I call your attention to a detail. My objective is to get Mr. Cather released and not charged with homicide. It's likely that I could achieve it simply by telling the police about Mr. Fleming blackmailing you. At least that would divert them, but I don't intend or desire to do it. I owe you some consideration, since I learned of the blackmailing only through you. I'm obliged to you."

Ballou reached a hand to tap the package. "And there's this."

"Yours. I haven't accepted it. Nor shall I, until I have concluded with finality that you did not kill that woman. A blackmailer is not *ipso facto* a murderer. I'm obliged to you because we have spent four futile days trying to find someone with a likely motive and have failed. The motive you suggested for Mr. Cather fits Mr. Fleming admirably. A question. How soon after the first phone call from the blackmailer did you tell Miss Kerr about it?"

"Right away. A day or two later."

"Was it ever mentioned again? By you or her?"

"Yes. She asked two or three times if it was continuing. I told her about the phone call in December. The last time she asked me was in January. Around the middle of January."

Wolfe nodded. "She knew it must be her brother-in-law, and she told him it must stop, and he—"

"Better than that," I cut in. "She was going to tell on him. Tell her sister. He might rather have called it off than kill her, but he would rather kill her than have his wife know. He may not be *ipso facto* a murderer, but *ipso* Archie Goodwin he is."

"Mr. Goodwin is sometimes a little precipitate," Wolfe told Ballou. "He has seen and spoken with them—Mr. and Mrs. Fleming. At length." He pointed to the package. "That money. If I earn it I want it, but you can't engage me now. My purpose is to clear Mr. Cather; yours is to prevent disclosure of your name. If I can serve your purpose without damage to mine, I shall. When you go, take the package; here in my safe it might affect my mental processes. There is—"

"What are you going to do?" Ballou demanded. Demanding again.

"I don't know. Mr. Goodwin, Mr. Panzer, Mr. Durkin, and I are now going to confer." He looked at the clock. "It's nearly midnight. If you don't want two more men in on your secret, go."

and great work on besides Orrie Cather, I
had a slew of Flatbush fingerprints to look for
— from the apartment, of course, so it would
take hours. With luck by bedtime he would

11

At one o'clock Friday afternoon I was on a chair in
a hotel bedroom, at arm's length from an attractive
young woman in the bed.

Various possible approaches had been discussed in
the Thursday night conference that went on for more
than two hours. Two of them—get a picture of him
and show it to the General Delivery clerks at the
Grand Central Station post office, and find out if he
had been spending more money than he should have
had—were discarded offhand because they could only
confirm the blackmailing, and that was regarded as
settled.

An obvious one was where had he been Saturday
morning, but we weren't ready for that. If he was
open, he was open. If he had an alibi, cracking it
could and should wait until we had some kind of
leverage on him.

Get three pictures of him, somehow—one for Saul,
one for Fred, and one for me—and do the neighborhood again, to dig up someone who had seen him
Saturday morning. The cops had of course been at
that for four days, with pictures of Orrie. Fred was
for it, and Saul was willing to try, but Wolfe vetoed it.
He said we had tolerated banality long enough.

Give it to Cramer. Saul suggested it, and he had a
case. We could give him the crop, all except Ballou's
name. It wouldn't hurt us any, certainly it wouldn't
stop us, and it would give Cramer something to think

about, and even work on, besides Orrie Cather. If they had a few of Fleming's fingerprints in their collection from the apartment, or even one, it would open it up good. Wolfe wouldn't buy it. He said it would be inept to have the police move in on Fleming before we did; for one thing, they would probably pry X's name out of either Fleming or his wife, and we weren't giving it even to Saul and Fred. The fifty grand wasn't there in the safe to affect his mental processes, but he knew where it was.

I made the suggestion that gave him a bright idea. There was nothing bright about the suggestion; it was simply that I would bring the Flemings to the office for some conversation with Wolfe. As we all knew, many people had said more to Wolfe than they had realized they were saying, and why not give them a chance? Saul and Fred could be at the peephole in the alcove, and then we would have another conference. I was the only one who had ever seen them. Saul and Fred were all for it, but Wolfe sat and scowled at me, which was natural, since it would mean another session with a woman. He sat and scowled, and we sat and looked at him. After half a minute of that he spoke to me. "Your notebook."

I swiveled and got it, and a pen.

"A letter. The regular letterhead. To Mr. Milton Thales, care of Mr. Barry Fleming, and the address. Dear Mr. Thales. It is a truism that people who have a sudden substantial increase in income often spend it, comma, or part of it, comma, on luxuries which they have previously been unable to afford. Period. It is possible that you are an admirer of orchids, comma, and that you would like to buy a few orchid plants with part of the five thousand dollars of extra income you have received during the past four months. Period. If so, comma, I shall be glad to show you my collection if you will telephone for an appointment. Sincerely yours."

I tossed the notebook on the desk. "Wonderful," I said. "It will bring him but not her. *Maybe*. If it goes to his home address and she's there when it's delivered but he isn't, it may bring her but not him. Statistics show that seventy-four per cent of wives open letters, with or without a teakettle. Why not send it to the school?"

"It's two o'clock Friday morning," Saul said. "He wouldn't get it until Monday."

Wolfe growled. I said, "Damn it."

"It's a beautiful idea," Saul said. "It will get him sweating before he comes, and that will help, and he'll have to come. Even if he didn't kill her, he'd have to come. But may I offer an amendment?"

"Yes."

"The letter might read something like this—your notebook, Archie? Dear Mr. Thales. As you know, comma, I was Isabel's closest friend, comma, and we told each other many things. One thing she told me was how you got that five thousand dollars and how she felt about it. I haven't told anyone else because she told me in confidence—no, change that. Change 'because she told me in confidence' to 'because I promised her I wouldn't.' Then: You may want to show your appreciation by giving me part of the five thousand, comma, at least half of it. I will expect you to bring it not later than Sunday afternoon. I work evenings. My address is above, and my phone number is so-and-so. It will be signed by Julie Jaquette. I suppose she should write it; I doubt if she uses a typewriter."

Fred said, "And he croaks her and then we've got him."

Saul nodded. "He would if we let him, and if he killed Isabel Kerr. If he's had practice." To Wolfe: "I just think that might be quicker than coming from you. I couldn't get her to do it, I'm a rat, but Archie could."

"Sure," I said. "I'll tell her I'll send orchids to her funeral." I looked at Wolfe. "You wished her well."

"So you demur," he said.

"No, sir. I like it. I merely remark that selling her

won't be easy, and if she buys it we can't let her out of our sight for one second, and what if she won't cooperate on that? Nobody suggests anything to her. She said so."

"But you like it?"

"Yes. If it misses we can blame it on Saul."

"Blaming is fatuous. The wording of the letter is important. Read it."

So that's why, at one o'clock Friday afternoon, I was settled in a comfortable chair in a bedroom on the ninth floor of the Maidstone Hotel, on Central Park West in the Seventies. Julie Jaquette, in the bed, was not stretched out; she was propped up against three pillows, drinking her third cup of coffee, having cleaned up the toast and bacon and eggs and muffins and strawberry jam, while I explained about the blackmailing caper, including Thā-lēz of Miletus, but not including Ballou's name. It was a nice big room, made even nicer by the clusters of *Vanda rogersi* which I had brought, in a vase on the over-the-bed table. She had stuck one of the flowers in the front V of what she had on, a light blue thing with sleeves and no frills. She had said she was no treat in bed in the morning, but actually she wasn't at all hard to look at. Clear-eyed and fresh and kind of hard-boiled wholesome.

"Poor Isabel," she said. "You can't beat that for lousy breaks, a blackmailer for a brother-in-law and a murderer for a pet. My God."

"And a heehaw for a friend," I said.

"She only had one real friend. Me."

"Right. I call you a mule only professionally. If I was being personal I would call you kitten or snuggle-bunny or lamb. Profess—"

"Do you realize this is a bed? That I could reach out and grab you?"

"Yeah, I'm watching every move. I call you a mule professionally because the minute you heard that your friend Isabel had been murdered you decided Orrie Cather had done it and you won't budge, not even when the third smartest detective in New York gives you ten to one. It would—"

"Who are the two smartest?"

"Nero Wolfe and me, but don't quote me. It would take an hour to explain why all three of us have crossed Orrie off, and even then you might not budge. But now we think we know who did kill her. The blackmailer. Barry Fleming. Her sister's husband."

She put the coffee cup down. "Huh. You got reasons?"

"If you mean evidence, no. But if there's any other good candidate we can't find him or her, and we have tried hard. Barry Fleming is perfect. Obviously Isabel told Stella who was keeping her—X, to you—and Stella had told Barry, since he couldn't blackmail him unless—"

"I may be a mule, but I can count up to two and I can say the alphabet backward."

"A mule *would* say it backward. When X told Isabel he was being blackmailed, she knew it must be Barry. She tried to make him stop, but he wouldn't. Finally she told him she was going to tell Stella; she had probably threatened to before. That was Saturday morning. She told him she had definitely decided to tell Stella when she saw her that evening, and he killed her. Count up to two."

"Don't wear me out." She shoved the table away, and the vase swayed, and I jumped to save it. She slid down in the bed, tossed one of the pillows on the floor, and propped her head on the other two. "You're quick," she said. "Graceful, too. You could make a chorus line easy. Leave your name with the girl at the desk. Have you explained all this to the cops?"

"No."

"Why not?"

I thought it unnecessary to tell her about the fifty grand. "Because they like Orrie and they've got him, and we have no evidence. Not one little scrap. The reason I'm telling you, we thought you might be willing to help. You do want the man that murdered her to get it, don't you?"

"You're damn right I do."

"Then you might help. You could write Fleming a letter, calling him Thales, and telling him you want the five grand he got from X—or most of it. Tell him that Isabel told you everything, maybe even hint that you think he killed her and you know why. Of course he would have to see you, and also, if he killed Isabel, he would have to kill you, and it would be a cinch for us to arrange to have evidence of *that*. So we'd have him. Happy ending."

She laughed, and she was such a good laugher that I caught it and joined in. When she had it under control she said, "You're not married, are you?"

I shook my head. "Nope."

"Never?"

"Nope. I've asked at least a thousand."

"I'll bet. I was once, and what a year *that* was. Do you know what I'm going to do when you leave?"

"Nope."

"I'm going to stand at the window and look out, and think it's a damn shame that it simply won't work. Anyway, if I'm going to get killed, all you'd get out of it would be a trip to the cemetery. This letter. Exactly what do I say?"

I waved a hand. "Forget it. A gag is for a laugh, and I got it."

"Nuts." She aimed a finger at me. "Listen, you. ZYXWVUTSRQPONMLKJIHGFEDCBA. You came to deal me in. Don't spoil it with a phony shuffle. Ten to one, twenty to one, you and Nero Wolfe wrote it out and you've got it in your pocket. Let's see it."

She would have had me if I hadn't taken the trouble to memorize it. "Thank God," I said, "you decided not to marry me. I'd get a Charley horse just trying to keep up. All right, we did discuss what the letter might say. But if you write it and I mail it, the minute he gets it you're a sitting duck. To-morrow's Saturday. If you write it now and I mail it, he'll get it tomorrow morning. He might move fast and he might try anything. At ten o'clock tomorrow morning I'll be here, outside in the hall, and Saul Panzer, the rat, will be down in the lobby. When you leave, we leave with you, and we stick, and you don't try any dodges just to show that you know what men are for and what they're not for. At the Ten Little Indians we'll be there, and so will Fred Durkin, and one of us will be here, in the hall, all night. And so on until something happens."

"That's screwy," she said. "How could anything happen with all you heroes right there?"

"Leave that to us. We can't arrange details until we see how he reacts. You're willing to give it a try?"

"Certainly. The way you danced me in, I have to. Anyway, I want to. Nobody has ever tried to kill me, and it will make me feel important. All my life I have wanted to feel important."

"So has everybody else. But it must be understood that you will follow sugges—you will obey orders. You'll do exactly what you're told. What do you swear on, the Bible?"

"No, some of the men in it are awful, and so are the women. We'll shake." She offered a hand.

It was a purely professional contact, but it was a fact that she had nice hands, and I said so. "Before we go to work on the letter," I said, "I should mention the possibility that Stella may open it and read it. That would make it a different situation, but maybe even a better one. Anyhow, tomorrow is Saturday and he'll probably be there. Now the letter. We had the idea of addressing it to Milton Thales, care of Barry Fleming, but that would just be a stunt. Mr. Wolfe likes stunts. Would you call him Barry or Mr. Fleming?"

"I've never seen him. Mr. Fleming."

"Okay. On the hotel stationery. Dear Mr. Fleming. As you know, I was Isabel's closest friend, and we told each other everything. She told me all about Milton Thales, and how you got that five thousand dollars, and how she felt about it. She also told me she was going to tell her sister, and that she would tell you first that she was going to tell her. That didn't surprise me, I knew her so well. But I wonder if that had anything to do with what happened to her, and I would like to know. One thing, considering how you got that five thousand dollars, I don't think you should keep it. I think you should give it to me and I'll give it to some charity. I expect to hear from you soon. I live at this hotel. Sincerely yours. Of course the wording can be changed, as long as the points are covered."

She was frowning. "That's a lot of lies for one short letter."

"Only one lie, that she told you. The fact is, *I* told you. All the rest is true. You do wonder if that had anything to do with what happened to her, and you would like to know. You're sticking your neck out to find out."

"I'm sticking my neck out because you smooth-tongued me into it. I never thought—"

"Whoa. Back up. I couldn't possibly smooth-tongue you into doing something you didn't want to do. Do you *want* to do it?"

"Oh, damn you, yes." She sat up, and the orchid fell out of the V. "Go in the other room and I'll come in ten minutes. I can't write in bed."

I timed her. It was twenty-two minutes. She wasn't perfect.

12

Back in 1958, eight years back, a man named Simon Jacobs should not have been stabbed to death and his body dragged behind a bush in Van Cortlandt Park, but he was, and Nero Wolfe and I would never forget it. We should have known it might happen and taken steps, and we hadn't. Once is enough for that kind of goof, which accounts for the fact that I did not arrive at the Maidstone Hotel at ten o'clock Saturday morning. I arrived at nine-thirty. Mail deliveries in New York are terrible, but there was one chance in a billion that the postman would get to 2938 Humboldt Avenue extra early that one day, and the subway is rapid transit.

A hotel manager doesn't like it if a guest tells him she wants to post a guard outside her door because she expects to be murdered, so we hadn't bothered the Maidstone manager. Instead, we had invited the hotel dick, I mean security officer, up to the room, and Julie Jaquette had told him that a man had been annoying her, and he might even take a room in the hotel, and she didn't want any trouble. It helped that he had heard of Nero Wolfe and Archie Goodwin and that I slipped him a double sawbuck. He even offered to supply a chair.

Since I had brought the *Times* and a magazine along, I didn't have to invent games to pass the time. There were DO NOT DISTURB signs on the doorknobs of her suite, and the chambermaids skipped them. The traffic was light all morning. I hope I'm not a snob, but I decided that on the whole I preferred the tenants of the seventh floor of 2938 Humboldt Avenue to those of the ninth floor of the Maidstone. They had all looked worried too, more or less, but you had the feeling that you could stand hearing about theirs. Of course people in hotels aren't like people at home. I was deciding why that was so when one of her doors, the one to the bedroom, opened enough to let her head through, and she stuck it out and asked, "What do you want for lunch?"

I looked at my watch. Ten minutes to twelve. "I'll make out," I said. "A bellboy will be up later. All arranged."

"Huh. You're slipping. I'm ordering breakfast. What if he fixes the waiter and poisons it? You'll have to taste. What for you?"

"Just double your breakfast."

"I always have bacon and eggs. I'll open the other door."

She did. In a minute it opened a crack, but I didn't go in. Remember Simon Jacobs, and have a look at the waiter while he's still out in the hall. It sometimes happens that the difference between being sensible and being silly doesn't depend on you at all, it depends on something or somebody else. That time it was silly to wait out in the hall for a look at the waiter. When he came, at half past twelve, wheeling the chow wagon down the hall, I watched him to the bedroom door and then went to the other one.

The meal was served in the bedroom, with her in bed and me at a table the waiter brought in. She was in the same blue thing as the day before, which made me feel at home. Since Fritz never fries eggs, they made me feel away from home. We talked about Isabel, or rather she did. She had been trying to figure out a way to persuade her to give up the idea of getting married, and she thought she might possibly have made it. She explained that the reason there is no such thing as a good husband is that there is no such thing as a good wife and vice versa, and how are you going to get around that? We had got to the muffins and jam, and she was telling me how right Isabel had been to realize that she wasn't cut out for show business, when the phone rang, and she twisted around and reached for it.

The first thing she said was "Hello," and the second thing she said was "Yes, Mr. Fleming, this is Julie Jaquette," and I beat it to the other room and got at the phone, but I didn't hear much. He said, "Would two o'clock be all right?" and she said, "Half past two would be better," and he said, "All right, I'll be there," and that was it. As I re-entered the bedroom she asked if I had heard it, and I said yes and went to my table.

"I suppose," she said, "we'd better decide what charity I'll give it to. Or have you arranged that too?"

"That's not funny." I poured coffee. "I'm going to call you Julie."

"That's not funny either. Will be bring his own ashtray?"

"Sure. I assume he's coming here."

"Yes."

"I told you we couldn't arrange details until we see how he reacts. He certainly doesn't intend to come and have them phone up, and take the elevator, and walk in and do you, and walk out again."

"Then you can be in the closet. Or in here." She pushed the over-the-bed table away. "I'm going to dress up for this. My best. Take your coffee to the other room."

I obeyed. For a hotel the sitting room wasn't bad—dark green carpet and light green walls, with the regulation chairs and an oversized couch, and a big window that looked down on Central Park. After I finished the coffee I went to the window for a look out. It was Saturday, but also it was February, and there wasn't much stirring in the park. There was still some snow under the bare trees and along the top of the park wall, but you could call it white only because it wasn't black.

Julie, when she came, was black—a plain black tailored dress with half-sleeves and no trim to speak of. I know when things fit, and no wonder she called it her best, the way it fitted. I said so and then took her to the window. "I'm about to give an order," I said. "See that stone wall over there? What time do you get home from work?"

"About half past one. I finish my last turn at one."

"Fine. The park will be empty. So when you get home tonight you turn on the lights and come and stand here to look out at the park, and the man behind the stone wall with his rifle resting on the wall pulls the trigger, and if he's any good at all down you go. Therefore you do not come and stand here and look out. You lower the blind and close the drapes before you leave for work. That's an order."

"It's a damn silly one. Way up here? At that angle? Go get a rifle and try it. You couldn't even hit the window."

"The hell I couldn't. Before I was twelve years old I got many a squirrel with a twenty-two in trees nearly this high. Are you going to obey orders or not?"

She said she would, and we went and sat on the couch and discussed the operation. She wanted to handle it with me in the other room listening, and she had a reason: if I sat in I might say something she wouldn't like but couldn't object to with him there. It got a little warm, and at one point she threatened to bow out and I could see him downstairs, but finally it was agreed that I would be present, seen but not heard unless I thought it was absolutely essential. We were barely on speaking terms when the phone rang and she was informed that Mr. Fleming was below and wanted to come up. I stayed on the couch. I stayed put when the knock sounded and she went and opened the door and he entered. Seeing it and not knowing, you would have thought it was she, not he, who needed watching. She turned to close the door, and he turned to keep her in view, and it wasn't until she had passed him and he turned again that he saw me.

He spoke. He said, "Oh," but didn't know he was saying it. Then he stood and stared. Julie faced him and said, "I believe you have met Mr. Goodwin. I'll take your coat."

His mouth opened, but no words came. He tried again and managed it. "I thought you—this would be private."

She nodded. "I suppose you would rather have it private, but I thought I'd better be careful with a —with you. Have you got the money?"

He was having trouble with his eyes. He wanted them to stay on her, but they wanted me in. "I'm afraid," he said, "there's a serious misunderstanding. I'm afraid Isabel told you some things that weren't true. I'm afraid—"

"Nuts. Milton Thales. Thā-lēz. I know exactly how you got it and who you got it from. The only reason I haven't told the cops is because Isabel wouldn't want me to. She would want me to make you cough it up, and that's what I'm doing. I think she would also want me to tell her sister, because she intended to, and I think I ought to, but first I want the money. Have you got it?"

"No. Honestly, Miss Jaquette, really—"

"Nuts." She whirled. "What do you think, Mr. Goodwin?"

Formal, yet. She could have made it Archie. "I think you're wasting your time," I said. "I think I ought to call Inspector Cramer and tell him to come and get him. I suggest Cramer because he handles homicide and he may be interested." I rose and went to the stand where the phone was and lifted the receiver and started to dial.

Fleming's voice came, not a yell, but loud. "No!"

I turned. "No?"

"I'll give you the money." From that angle the light was bouncing off his cheekbones. "I couldn't get it today, the bank's closed. I'll bring it Monday."

I cradled the phone. Julie said, "All of it. Five thousand."

"Yes. Of course." His eyes went with me back to the couch, and then to her. "What you said—I don't think Isabel would want you to tell my wife, now that she—I'm sure she wouldn't. Promise me you won't. I'm going to give you the money."

Julie shook her head. "I'm not promising anything."

"Promise me you won't tell her before Monday. We can talk about it Monday. I can tell you why—we can talk about it."

I spoke because I considered it absolutely essential for him to know he had some time to play with. "I'm here too," I said. "I can't speak for Miss Jaquette, but I can for me. I promise positively to say nothing to your wife until after you return the five grand, provided it's Monday. Then we'll see."

"All right," she said. "Archie's promise is no good without mine. I promise too."

He put his hat on. If he had known he was putting it on, in a lady's room with the lady present, he would have been shocked. He wanted to say something more, but didn't know what, and he turned, slow and stiff, and headed for the door. Then he forgot his manners again. When he shut the door he left it open a crack. Julie went and pushed it shut and then came to me and asked, "How was I?"

"Terrible. You called me Mr. Goodwin and then Archie. He'll think you don't know your own mind."

"I think you don't know yours. I thought the idea was to fox him into killing me."

"Into trying to. It sounds better, now that I've got acquainted with you."

"All right, you've hashed it. I knew damn well you should have stayed in the other room. Now he knows he'd have to kill you too."

"He does not. Didn't I explain that? Sit down." I

patted the couch, and she sat. "It's simple. He thinks they can't get him for the murder without you because you're the only one who can supply the motive. Of course you wouldn't go on the stand and swear that Isabel told you she was going to tell him that she was going to tell Stella about the blackmail, but he thinks you would. He also thinks you will tell Stella, not before Monday, but soon after, and apparently that bites him even deeper, I don't know why; he must see more in her than I do. So you're a double-breasted danger, but I'm not. I'm only hearsay. As he sees it, I can only tell what you told me, but you can tell what Isabel told you herself. That's equally true for the witness stand and for Stella. She would probably believe you, but not me. We haven't got a single item of evidence to connect him with either the blackmail or the murder, but if he hands you five thousand bucks' worth of currency, *that* would be evidence. He never will. So you'll have to be removed, but I'm just a nuisance. Sorry."

"Huh. You *have* dealt me in."

"Up to your neck. I apologize for one thing. I should have made it clear that once you were in you couldn't get out. I apologize."

"I don't want out. I think he killed her."

"Certainly he did."

"What do we do now?"

"Whatever you had on your program, if there's room for company. It's three o'clock Saturday afternoon. If you go out, Saul Panzer is downstairs and we'll escort you. If you stay in, I'll be in the hall."

"Do you play gin?"

I said I did, and that took care of the afternoon, after I went down and told Saul he was done for the day, provided he would call Fred and tell him to be at the Maidstone entrance or in the lobby at five minutes to seven, prepared to spend the night in the ninth-floor hall after our return from the Ten Little Indians. The three hours of gin cost me $8.75. She wasn't so good and I'm not so bad, but since she was going to drop ten bucks to Saul on their bet I thought it only fair not to bear down. She was a neater shuffler than anyone I know except Lon Cohen. We knocked off at six o'clock for a bite to eat, sandwiches and coffee from room service, and for her to change.

I had seen quite a few of the Manhattan spots, mostly with Lily Rowan, but had never been inside the Ten Little Indians, on Monarch Street. I spent that evening not only inside, but partly way inside, in Julie's dressing room, which was about six by eight, par for a headliner in a place with a four-dollar cover charge. When she was on I went out to the battlefield and stood in the rear at one side. Fred was at the center, near the door. Julie earned her pay, probably about a grand a week, maybe more. This is not a scout report on an artiste, so I'll let it go at that; she earned her pay. The Saturday-night mob certainly thought so; they loved her. For that matter, so did I, but on different grounds. One of them loved her so much that around midnight he somehow made it to her dressing room, so boiled that I had to be careful not to tip him over.

There was no taxi problem when the three of us made our exit into the windy winter night, because Julie had a standing arrangement with a hackie for a quarter past one. During the ride uptown she and Fred resumed a discussion they had started on the ride downtown; they had agreed it would be a good idea for her to rent one of his four children for the summer and were considering which one and the price. Knowing him, I hoped she didn't think he meant it, and knowing her, I hoped he didn't think she did.

When we stopped at the curb at the Maidstone, the doorman was right there to open the door, and we piled out and the cab rolled on. I wasn't going in; I was to relieve Fred up in the hall at ten o'clock and should have been in bed two hours ago. We were grouped on the sidewalk, Julie in the middle, when the first shot was fired. I reacted to the sound, a loud, sharp crack, and Fred reacted to the bullet, though I didn't know that immediately. He went down. I'm not certain whether the second shot was fired before, or after, or while, I was flattening Julie. If you think it would have been better manners just to cover her, I agree, but to do that properly you have to know which direction the bullets are coming from. I did cover her when I had her down. I twisted around to look up, and the damn fool doorman was standing there with his mouth open, staring across the street. No more shots. I ordered Julie, "Stay flat, don't move," and got to my feet, and as I did so Fred said, "The bastard hit me." He was on one knee, with his other leg stretched out, propping himself with a hand. I asked him where, and he said his leg. The doorman said, "Over there by the wall, I saw it." Julie said nothing. Good for her. I looked around. A bellboy was coming out of the hotel. A man and woman had stopped at the corner and were gawking. In the other direction, uptown, a bull was coming on the trot. I told Julie again to stay flat, and hopped. He just might be crazy enough to stick, thinking she might get up and he could try again. I had to scramble to see over the wall. There was practically no light behind it, but there was enough snow to spot anything as big as a man, and he wasn't there. When I got back across, the cop was bending over Fred and telling the bellboy to phone for an ambulance. Julie hadn't moved. I helped her up, told Fred I would be back, and started for the entrance with her. The cop said wait, he wanted names, and I told him he had heard me say I would be back, and went on. The desk clerk and the elevator man were there, and the clerk went and got the key and the elevator man came and took us up. Julie was trying not to tremble, and succeeding, and I decided she didn't want my hand on her arm as she walked from the elevator to her door.

Inside, in the sitting room, she said, "I'll bet my

coat's a mess," and slid it off before I could move to help her.

"Yeah, rub it in," I said. "Someday I'll tell you what a fine brave plucky game girl you are, not a single squawk, but now I'm busy. If it had been two feet to the left and a foot higher, you would now be meat. Luck, that's all, just pure luck, and I'm supposed to know what I'm doing. I'll go down and see about Fred. When I come back up you will be packed."

"Packed?"

"Right. What we call the South Room in Nero Wolfe's house, the one above his, has three windows facing south. Very nice in winter. You'll like it."

She shook her head. "I don't—I don't want to hide."

"Listen, snugglebunny. Kitten. Lamb. I have lost the right to give orders. Have I got to beg, for God's sake?" I went.

On the sidewalk a small audience had collected, a dozen or so. Fred was flat on his back, and the bell-boy was putting a cushion under his head. A woman was saying he'd get pneumonia. The cop and the doorman were across the street by the stone wall. I went and squatted by Fred and asked him which leg and where, and he said the left one a little above the knee and it probably got the bone, the way it felt. I asked what about blood, and he said there wasn't much, he had put his hand in and felt it, and he asked, "Is she all right?"

I said yes. "When I get back from the hospital I'm going to take her home with me. I don't want—"

"You're not going to any hospital. Take her now. The cop asked questions, but I don't know anything. Do I?"

"Sure you do. You know Nero Wolfe hired you to help me bodyguard her, and that's all."

"It's enough. Ouch. Take her now. I've been in hospitals before. Don't leave her alone. The sonof-abitch nearly got her with us right here. I only wish—"

He stopped because the cop had come. He wanted names, and I gave him some, Fred's and Julie's and mine, and nothing else. All I knew was that someone had shot a gun. He thought he would get tough but decided not to, and the ambulance came. I watched them load Fred and then went into the Maidstone and up to the ninth floor.

When I knocked on the door, Julie's voice came. "Is it you, Archie?"

"No. It's a Boy Scout."

She opened the door wide, and I stepped in. There on the floor were a big suitcase and a big bag. "I didn't send for a boy to take them down," she said, "because I thought you might change your mind."

I picked them up.

13

At nine o'clock Sunday morning I entered the kitchen, told Fritz good morning, got orange juice from the refrigerator, sat at my breakfast table, yawned, sneered at *The New York Times,* and rubbed my eyes. Fritz came with a piece of paper in his hand and demanded, "Were you drunk when you wrote this?"

I blinked at him. "No, just pooped. I've forgotten what I said. Please read it."

He cleared his throat. "Three-twenty A.M. There's a guest in the South Room. Tell him. I'll cook her breakfast. AG.'" He dropped it on the table. "I told him, and he asked who, and what could I say? And you will cook her breakfast in my kitchen?"

I took an economy-size swallow of orange juice. "Let's see if I can talk straight," I suggested. "I had four hours' sleep, exactly half what I need. As for telling him who she is, that is my function. I admit it's your function to cook breakfast, but she likes fried eggs and you don't fry eggs. Let's get to the real issue. There is one man who is more allergic to a woman in this house than he is, and you are it. By God, I *am* talking straight." I drank orange juice. "Don't worry, this woman is allergic to a man in *her* house. As for the eggs, poach them—you know, in red wine and bouillon—"

"Burgundian."

"That's it. With Canadian back bacon. That will

117

show her what men are for. Her usual hour for breakfast is half past twelve. I'm still willing to cook it if—"

He uttered a French sound, loud, maybe it was a word. He was at the range, with sausage. I reached for the *Times*.

Since Wolfe goes up to the plant rooms on Sunday morning only for a brief look, if at all, I supposed he would be down around ten o'clock. But it was still ten minutes short of ten when the sound of the elevator came, then his footsteps in the hall. I hadn't seen him since bedtime Friday evening, nearly forty hours ago. Instead of stopping at the office, the footsteps kept coming, and the swing door opened and he appeared.

"Indeed," he said. "You're alive."

I conceded it. "Just barely. Don't count on me for much."

"Who is the guest?"

"Miss Jaquette. Miss Jackson to you, Julie to me. She's alive too, but it's not my fault. She was shot at this morning, at half past one, in front of her hotel, from behind the Central Park wall. The sniper was not seen. Fred got it in the leg and is in Roosevelt Hospital. He was asleep when I phoned this morning. I phoned his wife when I got home last night. I also phoned Saul and told him to stand by. I brought Julie home with me because, with Orrie in the coop and Fred in the hospital, we're short-handed, and anyway I got tired of hearing bullets go by. She eats breakfast in bed, and Fritz will cook it and I'll take it up around half past twelve. That seems to cover it."

"The sniper was not seen."

"No, sir, but it was Barry Fleming. He reacted to the letter by coming to see her yesterday afternoon. That tagged him for blackmail, and the gunplay tagged him for murder. So all we need now is a little evidence. But I suppose you want a full report."

He said yes, and we went to the office. The Saturday mail was on my desk, unopened. I don't know why he does that, but I suspect that it's because he wants to show me that he won't butt in on my routine if I won't butt in on his. Fritz hadn't butted in either; my desk top was dustier than it gets in one day. I put my copy of the Sunday *Times* on it and sat, and proceeded to report. I gave it verbatim only in spots, the few that might have a bearing, thinking it unnecessary for him to know that she had asked me if I realized it was a bed, or that I had called her snugglebunny. Usually he opens his eyes and sits up when I finish, but that time he held it a full minute, and finally I spoke.

"If you're waiting for a comment, I have nothing to offer. I could say we know but can't prove we do, but that's obvious. As for last night, did he own a rifle, or did he get one, and if so where? Saul and I could dig up the answers, and then what? The first bullet either hit Fred's leg bone or went on through and hit the building, which is stone, and the second one presumably hit the building. Identifying them as coming from his rifle would take six experts, three on each side. If he had hit her and killed her that would be—"

"Pfui." He came erect. "That's mere futility. We have what we wanted, support for our surmise that he's a murderer. Is there any doubt now that we are going to extricate Orrie?"

"No."

"Then that is no longer of concern. Supposing that we could proceed to get proof, conclusive evidence, that Fleming killed Isabel Kerr, do we want to? If we get it, and give it to Mr. Cramer, what will happen?"

"Three things. One, they'll drop Orrie fast. Two, Fleming will be arrested, tried, and probably convicted. Three, they'll try to keep Ballou's name out of it but can't. Make it four. Four, you won't get another look at that package."

He nodded. "What did I tell him?"

"If you can serve his purpose without damage to yours, you will."

"Well?"

"Well, you can try. It's February sixth, with nothing coming in yet this year, and nothing in sight, and I know how much goes out, since I draw the checks. Do you want my opinion?"

"Yes."

"I don't see how we can possibly pull it. If we're going to spring Orrie, and we are, we're going to have to give them Fleming, with or without evidence, and he'll give them Ballou, and they'll have to see him. That's the trouble. Even if they play it tight and his name is kept out of the papers during the buildup, it's bound to get spilled in the courtroom, and he won't think he owes you anything. Neither will you. As you know, I am strongly in favor of income. I would hate to have my paycheck bounce. But you wanted my opinion."

"You misunderstood. I want your opinion on the risk, not on the feasibility. Could we conceivably jeopardize our purpose?"

"No. Orrie's as good as out now."

"Then there's no risk at all. The problem is to expose the murderer without—"

The doorbell rang, and I went to the hall, took a look, and stepped back in. "Cramer. Get Fritz. I'll go up and tell her not to sing 'Big Man Go-go' with the door open." I headed for the stairs.

By go-go, the door *was* open, though it had been shut when I passed by at nine o'clock. I lifted a hand to tap, but it wasn't necessary. She said, "My God, you're up and dressed." She was in a chair by a window. Her pajamas were light green with dark green stripes, and her feet were bare. Her hair was in all directions. I closed the door.

"I opened it," she said, "just to enjoy it. It's been years since I had a bedroom where I could leave the door open. I'm up because I woke up. I never stay in bed awake unless I'm reading or eating."

I had approached. "I'm afraid you'll have to wait a while on the eating. Inspector Cramer is here. He probably thinks you're here, since that cop saw you leave with me, but it's possible that we're not going to concede it. If we do, and if he insists on seeing you, we can say he'll have to postpone it because you're in a state of shock after last night, or I'll bring him up and you can get it over with. As you prefer. I thought I'd better ask you."

She took a swipe at the hair. "An inspector, huh?"

"Yeah. An old pal of ours. In reverse."

"I like to get things over with."

"Okay. He'll probably want to see you alone, and not in the office because he knows we have a hole to see and hear through. What do you want to keep you until breakfast? Will orange juice and coffee do?"

"Not if you have grapefruit juice."

"Certainly. Fritz will bring it up, and I'll bring Cramer up later. He may—"

"Here?"

"Sure. This room is bugged, he doesn't know that, and we'll be listening in. He may invite you down to the District Attorney's office, but you're not going. To take you with law he'd have to have a warrant, and he hasn't got one. Now the—"

"How do you know he hasn't?"

"I know everything except how to bodyguard a girl right. Now the main question. Do you remember the script? What we said last night?"

"What *you* said. Yes."

"Should we check it?"

"No. ZYXWVU—"

"Of course. I keep forgetting. Fritz will be up with the juice and coffee. Bolt the door. There's just a chance Mr. Wolfe will decide you're not here, to gain time, and Cramer will come hopping up to barge in. Once a cop's inside, he can move around and you don't touch him, but he can't bust doors in, or he'd better not. Don't answer knocks."

"Damn it," she said, "I ought to be sound asleep."

I said she could sleep all afternoon, and left.

Three paces inside the office I stopped to take in

an unexpected scene, homey and very appealing. I couldn't see Wolfe, at his desk, because the review-of-the-week section of the Sunday *Times*, spread wide, was hiding him. Cramer, in the red leather chair, had the sports section, spread just as wide. Having checked that Cramer had been admitted and was still there, I went to the kitchen, told Fritz the guest's name, asked him to take up grapefruit juice and coffee, and told him not to knock but give his name. Back in the office, Wolfe was still hidden. I crossed to my desk, sat and enjoyed the pleasant scene a couple of minutes, and then coughed. In a moment Wolfe folded the paper, put it on his desk, and spoke. To me.

"Mr. Cramer wishes to ask about that incident last night. Since you were there and I wasn't, I insisted on waiting for you." He turned. "Yes, Mr. Cramer?"

Cramer, having folded the sports section, put it on the stand. His eyes went to Wolfe. "I told you. I want to know why you had them guarding that girl, and who they were guarding her from. If you knew she was in danger, you know who fired those shots at her. Durkin says he doesn't know, but you do. I don't need Goodwin to tell me that. It's even possible he doesn't know, but you do. Assault with intent to kill is a felony, and you know who committed it, and I'm an officer of the law. Is that plain?"

Wolfe nodded. "Quite plain. It's also quite plain that your true interest is not assault with intent to kill, but an assault that did kill. Have you released Mr. Cather?"

"No. And I don't—"

"Are you prepared to release him?"

"No! I want an answer. Who fired those shots at that girl?"

Wolfe turned. "Do you know, Archie?"

"No, sir, I don't *know*. I could offer guesses, but not in the hearing of an officer of the law. Slander. I might guess Orrie Cather, but that's out because he's in the can, and unless—"

Cramer said a word, loud, which I omit because I suspect that some of the readers of these reports are people like retired schoolteachers and den mothers.

"Nor do I know," Wolfe said. "Mr. Cramer. Why not be forthright? You came here last Monday in the pretense that you hoped to get information that would strengthen your case against Mr. Cather, though you knew you would get none. Not from Mr. Goodwin. What you really wanted was to learn if my support of Mr. Cather was more than a gesture. What you want now is to learn if I have collected any evidence that will *weaken* your case against Mr. Cather. Why not be straightforward and ask me?"

"All right, I ask you. Have you?"

"Yes."

"What evidence?"

"I'm not prepared to divulge it."

"By God, you admit it. You admit you have evidence in a murder case and you withhold it."

Wolfe nodded. "It's a nice point. If I withhold evidence that would help to convict a man of murder I am obstructing justice, yes. But if I withhold evidence that would help to acquit a man, is that obstructing justice? I doubt if the point has ever arisen juridically. We could ask some—"

"Ask my ass. If you've got evidence that would help to clear Cather, it will help to convict someone else. I want it."

"That's nonsense. Thousands of men have been cleared by alibis, with no bearing on another's guilt. I have no evidence, none whatever, that would help to convict anyone of the murder of Isabel Kerr. I have a suspicion, a surmise, but that isn't evidence. As for the guarding of Miss Jaquette and the shots fired at her, how does that concern your effort to indict Mr. Cather? As Mr. Goodwin said, they couldn't have been fired by him, he's in custody. Under suspicion of murder."

"He hasn't been charged with homicide."

"You're holding him without bail. Consider a hypothesis. Suppose that Miss Jaquette had a private reason to fear that someone might try to do her violence, a reason she would not reveal, and arranged for protection, and got shot at. Do you think you could force her to disclose her secret, or could force me to?"

"Balls." Cramer was getting hoarse. He always did, with Wolfe. "You try being forthright. Will you give me your word of honor that your guarding her and the shots fired at her had no connection with the murder of Isabel Kerr?"

"Of course not. I suspect there was a connection. If so I would like to establish it—with evidence."

"You haven't already established it?"

"No."

Cramer got a cigar from a pocket, rolled it between his palms, stuck it in his mouth, and sank his teeth in it. But the rolling had loosened the wrapper, and a flap of it pointed up and touched his nose. He removed it, glared at it, hurled it at my wastebasket, and came close. It hit the edge and bounced to the floor. He aimed the glare at me and blurted, "All right, Goodwin. Where is she?"

I put a brow up. "You could mean Miss Jaquette."

"Yes, I could. You took her with you last night. And brought her here."

I nodded. "That's what Mr. Wolfe calls a surmise. You don't know I brought her here, just as I don't know who fired the shots. You're expecting me to stall, so I won't. She's up in the South Room. I was there chatting with her when you came."

"Now I'll chat with her. I'll go up." He left the chair. "I know the way."

"The door's bolted. We thought it might be better to hold off." I rose. "But you deserve a break. With a new Mayor and a new Commissioner, you probably need a break." I moved.

In the hall he stopped at the elevator, but I kept on to the stairs and he came. Policemen should keep fit. By the time he got to the second landing I had called to her and she had opened the door. She had changed to the blue thing and put slippers on. I pronounced names and asked if she had enough coffee and left them.

Taking it for granted that Wolfe had gone to the kitchen, I turned right at the bottom. He was there, in the only chair Fritz allows in his kitchen, with a seat ample for me but not for him, and had opened a certain cupboard door and flipped the switch. Fritz was on one of the stools at the big table, slicing a shallot, preparing for the poached eggs Burgundian, and I got the other stool.

Cramer's voice was coming from the cupboard. "I know that, I know you have. You made a full statement, and we appreciate that kind of cooperation. But that business last night is a new—element. Those two men were there, Archie Goodwin and Fred Durkin, for your protection, that right?"

JULIE: Yes.

CRAMER: You had arranged with Nero Wolfe for that protection?

JULIE: Yes.

CRAMER: When?

JULIE: Oh . . . I guess it was Saturday.

CRAMER: Why? Why did you need protection?

JULIE: I might as well tell you the truth.

CRAMER: Yes, that's always the best way.

JULIE: Between you and me, I didn't need protection. But one evening, I think it was Tuesday, I had come here because Nero Wolfe wanted to see me, and I met Archie Goodwin. And the next afternoon, Wednesday, I came again, and Archie took me up to show me the orchids, and we had a long talk. Are you sure this is confidential?

CRAMER: Yes.

JULIE: For God's sake don't tell him, but I simply flapped. What a man! I had to have him. So I—well, I made arrangements. He may not want you to know this, but he was there all day Saturday, in my hotel, from ten o'clock on. You may not approve, I suppose you're a married man, but when I want something I usually get it.

Wolfe was looking at me, and I was shaking my head. I had not suggested that. I was sorry I wasn't there to see Cramer glaring at her.

CRAMER: Do you mean to . . . are you saying that . . . you said you made arrangements. What arrangements?

JULIE: I told Archie a man was annoying me and I was afraid and I wanted protection day and night. You can understand why I wanted it day and *night*.

CRAMER: What's the name of the man who was annoying you?

JULIE: Aren't you an inspector?

CRAMER: Yes.

JULIE: Then you ought to listen better. Nobody was annoying me. I didn't need protection. I needed Archie.

CRAMER: If you didn't need protection, why did someone shoot at you, try to kill you?

JULIE: I've been thinking about that. Just because he hit Fred, there by me, that doesn't prove he was shooting at me. Maybe he was shooting at Fred. Or maybe he was just shooting at anybody. Like that boy in Brooklyn who shot some woman going by in a car. They get a kick—

CRAMER: Save it. I don't believe a word of it. Do you know what the penalty is for giving false information to an officer investigating a crime?

JULIE: No. What is it?

CRAMER: You can get five years.

JULIE: What crime are you investigating? Archie said you were investigating the murder of my friend Isabel Kerr, but you don't sound like it.

You only ask about me being protected and somebody shooting a gun. I must be thick.

CRAMER: No, Miss Jaquette, you're not thick. You're a damn good liar. Extra good. I hope you know what you're doing. Do you know that Wolfe and Goodwin are two of the slickest operators in New York?

JULIE: I don't know much about Nero Wolfe. I know a lot about Archie.

CRAMER: Well, they are. How much are they paying you?

JULIE: Paying me? Well. First I'm a liar, and now what am I?

CRAMER: That's what I'd like to know. Do you still think Orrie Cather killed your friend Isabel Kerr?

JULIE: I never said that.

CRAMER: You didn't have to. It was obvious from what you did say and put in your statement. Do you remember what you said?

JULIE: Certainly I do. I can say the alphabet backward.

CRAMER: Do you want to retract any of it?

JULIE: No. It was all true.

CRAMER: Then you still think he killed her?

JULIE: You ought to listen better. I told you I didn't say that.

CRAMER: You implied it strong enough. Don't forget we have your signed statement. Don't forget that.

Five seconds of silence except for a faint sound that could have been Cramer leaving his chair.

CRAMER: I warn you again, Miss Jaquette, giving false information to an officer investigating a capital crime is a felony. Do you want to reconsider it?

JULIE: No, thanks. You can leave the door open.

Another faint sound, the door opening. I slid off the stool, went to the cupboard and turned the switch, crossed to the door to the hall, and swung it open. Heavy footsteps were coming down the stairs. Cramer appeared, turned left, and passed the office door without looking in. He must have seen me as he was putting his coat on, but he didn't wave good-by. When he was out and the door shut, I turned and said, "That was ad lib, nothing like it in the script. I enjoyed every minute of it. You'd better start the eggs, Fritz, she must be hungry." I headed for the stairs and mounted the two flights.

The door was wide open. She was squatting on the floor, looking at the underside of the table. At the sound of my footsteps she turned her head, scrambled up, and said, "I'm looking for the bug."

"You won't find it there. It's not that simple. It came through fine."

"You heard it?"

"Sure. Why he called you a liar is beyond me. If ever I heard the ring of truth. How soon do you want breakfast?"

"Now. Right now."

"It's nearly ready. Get in bed and I'll bring it."

14

I don't mention everything, for instance phone calls that have nothing to do with progress or the lack of it. There had been two phone calls from Jill Hardy, one from Dr. Gamm, two from Lon Cohen, and three from Nathaniel Parker. But I mention the one from Parker that Sunday afternoon because what he wanted to do might have helped or hurt. He had decided he should make a habeas corpus play Monday morning to get Orrie bailed out, and it took Wolfe ten minutes to talk him out of it. It wasn't easy. Wolfe couldn't very well tell him that we were no longer worried about Orrie, that we now had another fish to fry.

Or maybe we did. When I went to bed Sunday night, after winning $1.25 from Julie at gin, there had been no discussion and no instructions, nothing. The Ten Little Indians was closed Sundays. Julie had had an afternoon nap, and I had had a long walk. Wolfe had had the *Times* and a book, and probably, while I was out, his weekly battle with television. That may occur almost any evening, when he has got disgusted with a book, but usually it's a Sunday afternoon, because that's when TV is supposed to be dressed for company. He turns on one channel after another, getting grimmer and grimmer, until he is completely assured that it's getting worse instead of better, and quits.

The only time he and Julie were together was at

the dinner table, and it was different from any meal at that table I could remember. Ordinarily Wolfe is perfectly willing to do most of the talking, with or without company, but that time, from the Neptune bouchées right through to the chestnut whip, he not only let the guest, a female guest, take over, he egged her on. He asked her questions, dozens of questions, about her work and her background and the people she knew. By the time coffee came, I had settled on the only possible explanation: he had decided that I didn't understand women as well as he had thought I did, and it was up to him to fill the gap. I could have told him that that kind of approach wouldn't help much, but apparently I was no longer regarded as an expert.

So I got a surprise when I entered the kitchen Monday morning and Fritz told me I was wanted, and I went up one flight and knocked and entered, and Wolfe said, "Good morning. Can that woman be trusted in a matter that requires adroit execution and full discretion?"

"You ought to know," I said, "after the quiz you put her through."

"I don't. Do you?"

"Yes. Adroit, yes. You heard her with Cramer. It would depend on how well she liked it, whatever it was. The discretion would also depend. She would never spill anything she didn't want to spill. She wouldn't talk just to hear herself."

"How much verity was there in what she told Mr. Cramer?"

"None at all. She couldn't think I'm what a man because she couldn't think any man is."

"Then we'll risk it. Ask Mr. Ballou to come at eleven o'clock. Tell him I'll need only ten minutes. Miss Jaquette must not see him. Can you make sure she doesn't?"

I said I could, and went up one flight to see if there was any sign of life there. It was only a quarter to nine, but she had gone to bed early—for her—and she might have opened the door to enjoy it. She hadn't. I had told her to buzz either the kitchen or the office on the house phone when she wanted breakfast, and to allow half an hour. I went down to the office and did the chores.

I didn't know if Avery Ballou was the early kind of president, and waited till a quarter to ten to dial the number of the Federal Holding Corporation. A woman answered, of course, and switched me to a man. He would submit my name to Mr. Ballou only if I told him what I wanted; that's one of the ways junior executives try to keep wise to what their seniors are up to. I finally persuaded him the name was enough and Ballou would want it, but there was a long wait before his voice came.

"Goodwin? Archie Goodwin?"

"Right. Mr. Ballou?"

"Yes."

"There has been a development in that matter we discussed Thursday evening, and we must tell you about it. Can you be here at eleven o'clock? Same address."

"This morning?"

"Yes."

"I'm afraid I can't. Is it urgent?"

"Yes. Eleven-thirty or twelve would do, but eleven would be better. It shouldn't take more than ten minutes."

"Hold the wire. . . . All right. I'll be there at eleven or shortly after."

If the junior executive had listened in, he must have been wondering what the hell could make Ballou jump like that, and wishing he knew.

After buzzing the plant rooms to tell Wolfe he was coming, I had a problem. Even if Julie was awake, it wasn't advisable to go up and tell her that a man was coming whom she must not see, so would she please stay in her room with the door shut. She was a fine brave plucky game girl, and she might go to my room, which fronts on 35th Street, and look out the window just to be helpful. It wouldn't be fair to tempt her like that, so I went to the kitchen, explained the situation to Fritz, and arranged with him. When the bell rang and I went to the door, he would go up to the second stair landing with the vacuum cleaner and camp there. If her door was open, he would vacuum the hall carpet. He said he couldn't vacuum that carpet for an hour, and I said he wouldn't have to.

Actually it was only eight or nine minutes. Wolfe came down on the dot at eleven, as he always does, and hadn't finished looking through the mail when the bell rang. I waited until Fritz was on his way upstairs, then admitted the caller, took his hat and coat, and followed him to the office. He stood and told Wolfe he didn't have time to sit.

"I like eyes at a level," Wolfe said. "It takes three seconds to sit."

Ballou sat.

"I'll make it as brief as possible," Wolfe said. "The first point, I am now satisfied that you didn't kill Isabel Kerr, because I know who did, barely short of certainty. Her brother-in-law. The blackmailer. The second point, there is no longer any question of achieving my primary purpose, to clear Mr. Cather. That is assured. The third point, I would like to earn that fifty thousand dollars. How can I earn it?"

"I thought that was understood. Keep me out of this mess. Keep my name out. I can't eat. I can't sleep. I have wanted a dozen times to call you, but I'm afraid to talk on the phone."

Wolfe shook his head. "It needs definition. Your name is known now. Five people know it—Mr. and Mrs. Fleming, Mr. Cather, Mr. Goodwin, and I. As for the last three, the best you can get is our assurance that we will disclose it to no one. As for Mr. and Mrs. Fleming, the best I could possibly do would be to create a situation which would make it highly unlikely that they would ever disclose it. I can't open their skulls and remove the cells where your name is filed. You see that."

"Yes."

"You would be the judge of the situation. I want to earn the money, not extort it. Now the fourth point, the reason I had to see you without delay. To proceed with any expectation of success, I must enlist help. I need the assistance of a woman named Julie Jaquette, or Amy Jackson, who was the friend—"

"I know the name. I know about her."

"From Miss Kerr."

"Yes."

"She doesn't know your name, and she doesn't need to. She calls you the lobster. I want to ask her help, without telling her your name, and I want to tell her that if we succeed she will receive fifty thousand dollars in cash. Will you supply it?"

Ballou frowned at him.

"You told me," Wolfe said, "that the fifty thousand was just a retainer and implied that there would be more if I served your purpose. I wouldn't want more. I'll get it done in a day or two, or not at all. I make it contingent on success, against precedent, to preclude any smell of extortion. Also, the prospect is dim. What are the odds against us, Archie?"

I didn't have to consider. "A thousand to one."

"This is pointless," Ballou said. "You know damned well I'm trapped. You told me you're my only hope. What's another fifty thousand, or ten times fifty? If you think she can help, all right. You don't seem—"

He wasn't interrupted; I was, by the sound of the vacuum cleaner. I rose and went to the hall, stood at the foot of the stairs, and heard no voices, just the vacuum cleaner. I was thinking the conversation was finished anyway and was turning to go and tell him where the door was, when he came. I was at the rack, ready with his coat, by the time he got there. His car was out in front, and I waited until he was in it and it was rolling, before going to the stairs and on up to the second landing.

Fritz was giving the carpet a play, and Julie, in pajamas and barefoot, was standing in the doorway, watching him. He had his back to her, pretending he didn't know she was there. I went and switched the vacuum off with my toe and spoke. "You might have waited until she was up."

"I *am* up," she said. "What time is it? I forgot to wind my watch."

A bellow came from below. "Archie! Where are you?" I called down where I was, and more bellow came. "Tell Miss Jaquette I want her!"

Ballou had been gone not more than three minutes, and already he had a situation created. Which I handled. I told Julie her breakfast couldn't be ready for half an hour and asked if she would consider having grapefruit juice and coffee in the office while Wolfe explained something to her. She asked why I couldn't explain it, and I said because Wolfe knew more words. She went to change, and I went down and thanked Fritz for helping out in a pinch, requested coffee for the guest, and poured a glass of grapefruit juice.

And after that handling, when I went to the office Wolfe said perhaps it would be better for him to discuss it with me, and then I would discuss it with her. I didn't try to talk him out of it; I just said no. I admit it was still in my gizzard that it was pure luck that she hadn't been ironed out while I was standing right by her. I'm all for luck, but you shouldn't crowd it. After what I had told her about lowering the blind and closing the drapes, I should have gone over for a look behind the wall before she got out of the taxi.

When she came down, not in the blue thing, in a dark green woolen dress, the tray was there on the stand by the red leather chair. She sat, picked up the glass and took a sip of juice, and said, "I'm all balled up. This will be the first time since I don't know when that I don't have breakfast in bed. It had better be good—I mean what you're going to explain."

Wolfe was regarding her, his lips tight. "I apologize. But we should lose no time. I say 'we' because I'm going to propose a collaboration. Have you all the money you want, Miss Jaquette?"

She had started the glass for her mouth but stopped it halfway. "Of all the dumb questions," she said.

"But not pointless. Nor impertinent. I need to know if a chance—a long one, but a chance—of making fifty thousand dollars would interest you. Would it?"

"That's even dumber."

"Would it?"

"You're asking me?"

"I am."

"Fifty grand in cash?"

"Yes."

"Less income tax."

"Not until you paid it. I suggest nothing; I state a fact: it would be in cash, and you would sign no receipt."

She sipped juice. "Do you know what I would do if I had fifty grand in one wad? I would go to school for four straight years. Or five." She sipped juice. "I suppose some college; I finished high school. I have a feeling there are a lot of things I ought to know that I don't know. I always have it. You say you're being serious?"

"Yes. There is a possibility of earning a hundred thousand dollars, and we would share it equally. It would come from the man who paid Isabel Kerr's bills—the man you call the lobster. He was here just now, and we—"

"He was *here?* You know him?"

"Yes. It was his third visit. He was here twice last week. He is a man of wealth and what is called standing. To you his name is X and will remain X. He fears that his name will become public in connection with what he calls his diversion and a sensational murder, and you and Mr. Goodwin and I will try to prevent it. If we succeed, he will pay. For that you have my word, he will pay. His fear is extreme. Shall I go on?"

She had put the glass down, not quite empty. "You *are* serious," she said.

"Yes."

"You mean it."

"Yes."

"All right, go on. How do we prevent it?"

"That's the question. Probably we can't, but possibly we can. If I go on I must tell you things that must not be repeated, and first you must answer two questions. Are you willing to help?"

"How? I don't see how I can help."

"You already have. You have established the identity of the blackmailer indubitably, and the identity of the murderer as a sound conclusion. If you can help with this, are you willing?"

She looked at me. I not only looked back, I nodded. She told Wolfe, "Yes, I'm *willing*."

"Do you engage to keep secret what I tell you in confidence?"

"Yes, that's all right. I can do that."

"Then you're a paragon. But there are things you have to know—for instance, that Mr. Goodwin and I learned X's name from Orrie Cather. Miss Kerr told his name to two people only, Orrie Cather and her sister. That may be safely assumed, because she didn't even tell you. Mrs. Fleming told her husband, so there are five people who know it. I will answer for three of the five: Mr. Goodwin, Mr. Cather, and me. There would be some question about Mr. Cather if he were going to be tried for murder, but he isn't. That leaves Mr. and Mrs. Fleming as the only sources for the disclosure of X's name. I am taking pains to make sure that it's clear to you."

"You sure are. Have I told you that I can say the alphabet backward?"

"You have told Mr. Goodwin and Mr. Cramer. So can I. Now for the fact that gives us our one chance in a thousand. There is one person who dreads the publication of X's association with Miss Kerr even more intensely than X does. Tell her, Archie."

I took five seconds, not to figure it, but to realize that I had never looked at it from that angle. I told Julie, "Stella. I told you Saturday how she reacted. Remember? She doesn't want a trial even if they get the right man. Of course, X's name would come out only in connection with Isabel." I looked at Wolfe. "Yeah. I'll be damned. But how?"

"That's what we need Miss Jaquette for." His eyes were narrowed at her. "Don't you want coffee? It's getting cold."

She picked up the glass and finished the juice, put it down, poured coffee, picked up the cup, and took a sip. She looked at Wolfe and shook her head. "I don't get it. What's so great about that fact?"

"The possibilities it presents. Suppose that Mrs. Fleming knows, or even strongly suspects, that her husband killed her sister, and knows why, and also knows that he may be arrested and charged at any moment, and later brought to trial. What would she do?"

"I don't know. I don't know her."

"What would she do, Archie?"

"I don't know either," I said, "*what* she would do. But I know she would do anything, no holds barred, to keep him or anyone else from telling the world about Isabel and X. She certainly wouldn't want it to get to a trial. I don't know how much she cares about *him*. If she cares enough, in spite of the fact that he killed Isabel, she might blow with him, or if she thinks he can stand the gaff and keep his trap shut, she might stick and fight. If she *doesn't* care enough about him, she might ship him off to China, or she might even bump him off. The one certain thing is that she would do whatever she thought she had to, to make sure, for instance, that Orrie wouldn't go on the stand as a witness for the prosecution and answer questions about Isabel. Or that X wouldn't testify

about the blackmail. Of course she has to be told about
the blackmail too. To make sure of that she would
blow up the courthouse if she could get her
hands on a bomb." I was looking at Julie. "So there
you are. You tell her what you told him in that
letter. It made him snipe at you with a gun. She
won't do that, but she'll certainly do something."

She was frowning. "Why can't you tell her?"

"She wouldn't believe me. You can tell her things
Isabel told you, but I can't. As you told him in the
letter."

"That was a lie, that letter."

"The only lie was that Isabel told you. What you
said she told you was true, and he proved it. Do you
know that Barry blackmailed X?"

"Certainly."

"Do you think there's any doubt that he shot at
you?"

"No."

"Do you think he would have tried to kill you just
because you knew about the blackmailing and wanted
the money, if he hadn't also killed Isabel? Remember,
I was there, and he knew what I was working on.
The murder. I think it would be fine for you to pick
up fifty grand, but also I understood that you wanted
the man who killed Isabel to be tagged. You said so.
Do you think there is any doubt that he killed her?"

"No."

"Then count up to two."

She picked up the cup and took a sip, found that
it had cooled enough, emptied the cup and put it
down, and said, "He wouldn't be tagged if they blow."

"No," I conceded. "But his number would be up,
and he wouldn't be here to name X. They'd find him
someday, and then we'd see. As Mr. Wolfe said,
probably we can't, but possibly we can."

"She lives in the Bronx."

"Right."

"Would I have to go there?"

"I hope not. This is the day he was to bring you

the five grand, and God knows where he is or what
he might try. I'm off of bodyguarding for a while."

"Here," Wolfe said. "Get her."

"I'll sit in," I told Julie, "if you think I won't hash it."

"What a man," she said, and poured coffee.

I swiveled, got the Bronx phone book, found the
number, lifted the receiver, and dialed, hoping she
was there and was answering the phone. She was. It
was her voice that said hello.

"This is Archie Goodwin, Mrs. Fleming. You may
remember, I was there a week ago today."

"I remember."

"Then you may remember that I said the police had
the wrong man and I was looking for the right man. I
have found him, and we want to tell you about him
and ask your advice about how to proceed. We know
you hope there won't be a trial, and we want to
discuss it with you. Will you come here, Nero Wolfe's
office? Now?"

Silence. It went on so long I thought she had gone,
but she hadn't hung up. I finally said, "Mrs. Fleming?"
but there was more silence.

At last her voice came. "Mr. Goodwin?"

"Yes."

"What's the address?"

I gave it to her.

15

It was a tough decision, and it took Wolfe a good
five minutes to make it. What about lunch? It was ten
minutes past twelve when I hung up after giving
Stella Fleming the address. Would she leave immediately, and how long would it take her? Lunch-
time has been, is, and will be a quarter past one. An
impossible situation. He sat and scowled at it for
five or six minutes, made his decision, and got up
and went to the kitchen. I followed him, since I eat
too. Julie had no problem, since her hedgehog omelet
and broiled sausage were about ready. The crisis was
licked good. Julie ate at my breakfast table, and
Wolfe and I made out on stools at the big table, with
sturgeon, smoked pheasant, celery, three kinds of
cheese, and spiced brandied cherries. Since it was a
snack, not a meal, the taboo on business didn't apply,
and we discussed the program. I thought Wolfe
should be present, and he thought he shouldn't, and
we let Julie decide it, and she voted with him. In
the alcove at the kitchen end of the hall there is a
hole in the wall with a sliding panel, and on the
office side the hole is covered with a trick picture of a
waterfall which you can see through from the alcove
side. Wolfe would be there on a stool. We were
unanimous on the other main point, that I should lead
the attack.

When she came, at twenty minutes past one, I
started the attack in the hall. A chair and a bench

are there, across from the rack, very handy, but she didn't put her handbag down when I was taking her coat, and I didn't like the way she was clutching it. Also I was still touchy about the bullets that had missed Julie through no fault of mine. So when, turning, she shifted the bag from her right hand to her left, I grabbed it. She tried to grab it back, but I stiff-armed her, perhaps a little rough, sidestepped, and opened the bag. She squeaked and came at me, and I pushed her again and got a hand in the bag, and it came out with something in it. She backed off and stood and panted, so I was able to look. It was a twenty-two Bristol automatic with a fancy carved butt, and it was loaded. I stuck it in my side pocket and held the bag out. "Sorry if I was rude," I said. "We had an event here once, and I frisk everybody."

She was trying hard to hold in, and I hoped she would make it. She had shrunk. Not only did she look even smaller than she had a week ago, but her face had positively shrunk. Her cheeks had been filled out, and now they weren't. She took the bag and said, "Give me that gun."

"It's not a gun, it's a toy. You'll get it back. As I say, I frisk everybody, and right now I'm glad I do. There's a woman here who is going to say things you won't like, and you're very impulsive. Her name is Julie Jaquette, and she was your sister's best friend. I believe you have met her—"

"I was my sister's best friend."

"You ought to know. Let's go in and sit down." I gestured. "That open door on the left."

I thought she was going to balk and she did too, but I had the gun and I could have carried her under one arm. She turned and clicked down the hall, and I followed. Two steps inside the office she stopped. I passed on by and went to Julie, who was standing by my desk. I took the pistol from my pocket and showed it to her. "This was in her bag," I said and turned and asked Stella, "Where does your husband keep his rifle?"

I don't think she heard me. I had moved up a couple of the yellow chairs, and she went to one and sat. Julie went and took the other one, and I returned the pistol to my pocket, sat at my desk, and told Julie, "You have met Mrs. Fleming."

She nodded. "That was in her bag? How did you get it?"

"Took it. It didn't fire those shots Saturday night." I eyed Stella. "Your husband shot at Miss Jaquette Saturday night, but missed. That's why I asked where he keeps his rifle."

She gawked at me. "What? My husband what?"

"He tried to kill Miss Jaquette. That's breaking it to you gently, Mrs. Fleming, there's much worse to come. I told you on the phone that I have found the right man. The reason Miss Jaquette is here is that she helped me find him. I guess the best way is to show you a copy of a letter she sent to your husband last Friday." I opened a drawer and got it. "She wrote it by hand; this is a typewritten copy. Shall I read it?"

She looked at Julie. "A letter you sent my husband?"

"Yes."

She put a hand out. "Let me see it."

I passed it over. She went through it fast and then read it again, slow. She looked at Julie. "What's it about? Who is Milton Thales?"

Julie looked at me, and she shouldn't have. She was supposed to be collaborating. I widened my eyes a little, and she went back to Stella. "Your husband," she said. "He is Milton Thales. I said in that letter that Isabel told me everything, but the one thing she didn't tell me was the name of the man who was paying her bills, so I have to call him X. You're the only one she told his name to, and—"

"She didn't tell me his name."

"She told me she *did* tell you. Isabel wasn't a liar."

That was more like it. What a girl. She was going on. "So when X got a phone call from a man who knew all about it and told X to send him money, a thousand dollars a month, to mail it to Milton Thales, General Delivery, and X told Isabel, she knew Milton Thales must be your husband. Because no other man could know what Milton Thales knew. Isabel knew you must have told your husband, and he—"

"I didn't tell my husband."

"You must have, because if—"

I cut in. "It's no good, Mrs. Fleming. That's nailed down. Your husband got that letter Saturday morning. At one o'clock he phoned Miss Jaquette at her hotel. At half past two he came in person. I was there with Miss Jaquette. He told us he hadn't brought the five thousand dollars he had screwed out of X because the bank wasn't open. He said he would bring it Monday. Today. What time did he get home Saturday night?"

No answer. She was staring at me.

"I know he got home late, because at half past one he was behind the wall in Central Park with either a rifle or a revolver, shooting at Miss Jaquette across the street when we got out of a taxicab. I brought Miss Jaquette home with me, here, so we don't know if he has tried to get in touch with her today, and we don't care. The point is, you did tell him X's name, and he did blackmail X, and Isabel knew it. That's settled."

She was clawing, but not at me. Her hands were resting on her knees, with the fingers curled, and she was scraping at her palms with her nails. "I can't believe it," she said, so low that I barely heard. She said louder, "I *can't* believe it."

"That's hard," I said, "but there's harder. This isn't nailed down, but it can be. As it stands now, it's what Isabel told Miss Jaquette. She not only told her about the blackmailing, she also told her that she was going to tell your husband that she had decided to tell you about it. When I first heard that, from Miss Jaquette, I wondered why the police were holding Orrie Cather instead of your husband, but then Miss Jaquette told me she hadn't told the police about the blackmailing at all. You can ask her why; I think it was because she didn't realize what it might mean. The police would have realized it. If she had told them about the blackmailing, all that Isabel told her, your husband would now be in jail, either along with Orrie Cather or instead of him, as a murder suspect. And when we tell them about his coming to see Miss Jaquette Saturday afternoon, and his trying to kill her that night, that will settle that. They'll get the evidence, for instance his movements the morning Isabel was killed, and he'll be booked for murder, and tried, and probably convicted. I told you on the phone that I have found the right man, and I have. Barry Fleming."

She had stopped the clawing and made fists, and had nodded three times as I talked—little involuntary nods, without knowing she was doing it, like the shake of her head when I told her that Orrie Cather might have been the one who was paying the rent. Now she whispered to herself, "That's why."

I didn't ask her why what, because I wasn't after evidence. You want evidence in order to prove something to the District Attorney or a judge or a jury, and that wasn't the program. Her "why" was probably something, or things, he had said or done—for instance, where he had said he had been, but hadn't, the morning Isabel was killed. Whatever it was, it made it a lot simpler than I had thought it would be. I had expected her to throw at least three fits, especially after finding the toy in her bag, and there she was whispering to herself.

Julie said, "You don't have to club her."

That was unnecessary, so I ignored it. What the hell, she had brought a gun, even if she had had no idea what for. Probably to mow me down if I called Isabel a doxy. "You may wonder," I told Stella, "why we wanted to discuss it with you. Since it's practically certain that he killed Isabel, why didn't we just tell the police? Of course we'll have to, but I haven't forgotten what you told me that day, that your sister's reputation was the most important thing in the world. I know nothing about your relations with your husband, but I thought it was possible you could do something. You might persuade him to go to the police and admit he killed her, and give an entirely different reason, some reason that would leave out the blackmailing and X and everything you don't want to come out. I don't know if that's possible, but I thought you ought to have the chance. We can't wait long, not more than a day or two. Say Wednesday morning."

"This is Monday," she said. She was getting her voice back.

"Right."

"I want that letter."

It had dropped to the floor when she started the clawing, and I had picked it up and put it on my desk. "It's just a typewritten copy," I said.

"I want it."

I got it, folded it, and handed it to her. She said, "The gun."

"When you leave. Whose is it, yours or your husband's?"

"It's his. He has medals for shooting." She put the letter in her bag, looked at Julie, and said, "You. It was people like you."

"Nuts," Julie said. "Anybody can say that to anybody. You mean I was bad for Isabel. I was a lot better for her than you were. I really loved her, but what about you? From what she told me, what—"

That did it. I had relaxed some, and she was so damned sudden. Her lunge at Julie was so fast that she was on her before I moved, and again it wasn't my fault that Julie didn't get hurt, at least some good scratches. Julie jerked her knees up, and with her feet off the floor the impact toppled her and the chair backward. Stella would have been on top, but by that time I was there and had her shoulders from behind. I pulled her off and up and pinned her arms, but she said, "I'm all right," and she was. The fit had gone as fast as it came. Julie scrambled up, took a swipe at her hair, and said, "You can club her, for all I care."

Wolfe's voice came, his coldest voice. "Mrs. Fleming."

We all turned. He was in the doorway. "Mr. Goodwin was too generous," he said, "giving you until Wednesday morning. Tomorrow morning at the latest. Get her out, Archie." He headed for his desk.

Stella's eyes followed him to his chair, then she looked around, evidently for her bag. I picked it up from where she had dropped it, put the gun in it, said, "I'll give it to you at the door," and moved, and she came.

16

At four o'clock Julie was in a chair by a window in the South Room, deeply interested, if you go by appearances, in a magazine, and I was standing in the doorway. We weren't speaking. I had asked her if I should ring the Ten Little Indians to tell them she wouldn't come this evening, or would she rather do it herself, and she had said neither one, she was going, and I had said she wasn't. The conversation had got very outspoken. At one point she had asked me to tell her Saul Panzer's number so she could call him and ask him to come and take her, since I didn't want to expose myself. At another point I said that I doubted if more than half of the customers would leave when they learned that she wouldn't appear. At still another she asked if I actually meant that she was being held there by force, against her will, and I said yes. By four o'clock it became apparent that we weren't going to be speaking.

Then the sound came of the elevator groaning its way up, and she raised her head to listen. When the groaning stopped and the sound came of the door opening above, she tossed the magazine on the table, got up, and walked. As she approached the doorway I politely moved aside, and she passed through, went to the stairs, and started up. She was either going to appeal to the owner of the house or help him with the orchids, and as far as I was concerned it didn't matter which. I went down the two flights to the office, called the Ten Little Indians, and said that Miss Jaquette had a cold and wouldn't be able to make it. I didn't say where she was because they might send someone with flowers and she didn't need any up there.

Being a warder, I couldn't go for a walk, and anyway I had to catch the news broadcasts every half-hour to learn if there had been any development worth reporting in a murder case, for instance that a man named Barry Fleming had been taken to the District Attorney's office for questioning in connection with the murder of his sister-in-law. There hadn't. I spent the two hours at the files and my desk, with the germination records. It helps, at a time like that, to have something to do that needs only one small corner of your mind, like entering on cards such items as the results to date of a cross between *Odontoglossum crispo-harryanum* x *aireworthi* or *Miltonia vexillaria* x *roezli*.

When they came down together in the elevator at six o'clock, I was too busy even to turn my head, but I became aware of a presence near my right shoulder, and a voice asked, "Can I help?"

So we were speaking. I said, "No, thanks."

"Did you phone?"

"Yeah, you have a cold."

"Has anything happened?"

"Yes. We have made up. Apparently."

"Oh, I never nurse a huff. Anyway, I knew you were right. I just wanted to see how mean you could get. One thing I could have said, I could have threatened to call a cop. Evidently the one thing you and Nero can't stand is for anybody to tell a cop anything. It's been more than four hours since she left. Damn it, what's she doing?"

That was the second time I had ever heard a woman call him Nero, but the other time it had been a gag. For Julie it was just natural. If she stayed two days and two nights in a man's house, and ate with him, and collaborated with him, and helped him with his orchids, it would have been silly to call him Mister. If she got the fifty grand and picked a college that wasn't too far away, I might drop in after she had been there a while to see what effect she was having. It was a cinch that she would have more effect on it than it would have on her.

I accepted her offer to help with the germination records.

At the dinner table Wolfe didn't repeat his performance of the day before. It was no longer necessary to quiz her, and he put her in her place by discussing the difference between imagination and invention in literature. She did get a word in now and then. Once when his mouth was full of sweetbreads she said, "You're talking over my head on purpose. Show me one thing in one book and ask me if it's imagination or invention and I'll tell you every time, and let's see you prove I'm wrong." That's no way to talk to a man who is doing his best to prepare you for college.

While Fritz was pouring after-dinner coffee in the office, Julie said, "I'd give a brand-new dollar bill to know what she's doing. What's her number? I'll call her."

"Yeah," I said.

She looked at Wolfe. "You get on my nerves because you haven't got any. You wouldn't give a rusty nickel to know what she's doing."

"Why should I?" he growled, and sipped coffee.

It was obvious that they had had enough of each other for a while, and when we had finished with the coffee I took her down to the basement. The basement has Fritz's room and bath, a storeroom, and a large room with a pool table. I had mentioned it to her, and she had said she would like to learn how to use a cue, and it might take her mind off of Stella Fleming, not to mention mine. But she didn't get her pool lesson. I had taken the cover off, and picked a cue for her, and racked the balls, when the doorbell rang. If I hadn't caught her arm she would have beaten me to the stairs, and she was right at my heels when I reached the hall and took a look at the front.

"My God," she said, "she hashed it." I stepped to the office door and told Wolfe, "Cramer." He looked up from his book and tightened his lips. I told Julie, "Go to the kitchen and stay there." The doorbell rang. Julie went, but not to the kitchen, to the alcove, where the hole was. I said, "If you sneeze, I'll boil you in oil," and went to the front and opened the door.

From the look Cramer gave me, he was set to boil me in oil whether I sneezed or not. That was all he had for me, the look. By the time I had his coat hung up he was at the office door, and when I got there he was already in the red leather chair and talking. He was saying, ". . . and you knew Barry Fleming fired those shots, and I want to know how you knew. You also knew Barry Fleming had killed Isabel Kerr, and I want to know how you knew that."

Good-by, fifty grand, I thought as I crossed to my desk. They had Fleming, and ten to one they would open him up, no matter how Stella had handled him. Maybe they already had.

Wolfe said, "You're fuming, Mr. Cramer."

"You're damn right I am."

"Then you're at a disadvantage. Don't you want to compose your mind?"

"I want you to answer questions!"

"If I know the answers. You say that I knew that Barry Fleming killed Isabel Kerr. I remind you that last evening I told you that I had no evidence that would help to convict anyone of that murder, that I had only a surmise. I repeat that. I still have no evidence. Have you?"

"Yes."

"Is Barry Fleming in custody?"

"No." Cramer's jaw was set. "Look, Wolfe. You've got what you wanted. You wanted to spring Cather, and you've worked it. He's clear. Now. I don't need evidence for Fleming, even if you've got it. I want some facts. I want to know if Barry Fleming fired those shots at Julie Jaquette, and if so why."

Wolfe's shoulders went up an eighth of an inch and down again. "Is that important? Important to you? Since you have him for murder—or have you? You say he's not in custody. If by any chance you think I have him here, waiting for you, I haven't. Is it—"

"You haven't got him here. He's dead."

"Indeed. By violence?"

"Yes."

A corner of Wolfe's mouth twisted up. "Mr. Goodwin and Miss Jaquette and I haven't left the house all day. So if you had any expectation—"

"Oh, cork it. He shot himself. About three hours ago. In the temple with a Bristol twenty-two automatic. It was his, he had a permit. And I want—"

"If you please. At his home?"

"Yes. I—"

"Was a policeman there? Had he been questioned?"

"No. If you—"

"Then how the devil do you know he killed Isabel Kerr? How do you know anything at all? Don't expect me to clear it up. I have told you twice, I have no evidence—"

"Goddammit, I don't need evidence. Not about Isabel Kerr. If you want it about him, okay. When he got home this afternoon, he and his wife had a talk, she says, and he wrote something and signed it. She went out to buy some groceries and was gone about half an hour and when she went back he was dead. How do I know he killed Isabel Kerr? She had it, what he wrote and signed."

He got a piece of folded paper from his breast pocket. "It has been checked with his handwriting, but the laboratory will verify it." He unfolded it. "It's his printed letterhead. Dated today." He read:

"To Whom It May Concern:
I hereby state and acknowledge that on Saturday, January 29, 1966, I struck my sister-in-law, Isabel

Kerr, on the head with an ashtray and killed her. It was not premeditated. I did it in an uncontrollable frenzy of anger and resentment. The resentment had been festering for three years. She had been living in great luxury and my wife and I were paying for it. All of my savings were gone, and with my small salary I would soon be at the end of my rope, but she would not listen to reason, and my wife was so devoted to her that she would not do what had to be done. That Saturday morning I tried once more to persuade Isabel, but could not, and I lost control of myself and hit her. I did not mean to kill her, but I do not expect forgiveness, even from my wife. My wife insists that I must write this so that she will have evidence of the circumstances of Isabel's death. She has given me no promises and I do not know what she will do with it.

Barry Fleming"

Cramer folded it and returned it to his pocket. "Naturally, the first thing you'll say, and I said, is that he doesn't say he's going to kill himself. No good-by. But they often don't. The gun was there on the floor, and the bullet went through his right temple at the right angle. She talked a little to the precinct man, but now she's out, completely out, under sedation. Of course we'll get at her later, but I'm not expecting much. I'm spilling this to you because it settles the Kerr thing and you might as well know it, but it doesn't settle everything. The shots that were fired at Julie Jaquette. You told me yesterday that you didn't know who fired them."

"I didn't. I still don't."

"That's a goddam lie."

"I lie only when I must. Now it isn't necessary. I told you yesterday that I suspected there was a connection between the murder of Isabel Kerr and the shots fired at Miss Jaquette, that I could guess, but I didn't know." Wolfe turned a hand over. "Mr. Cramer. There are certain details that I don't intend to divulge, and anyway, you don't need them now and would have no use for them. The murder is solved, and the culprit is dead. But not only are you a policeman with duties, you are also a man with the itch of curiosity, and furthermore I gall you. So I tell you this: I learned, no matter how, who was supplying the money for Isabel Kerr's luxurious way of life, and certain facts about it, and that led me to my surmise that Barry Fleming had killed her. I also learned, again no matter how, that Barry Fleming feared that Miss Jaquette would disclose certain facts which he thought she had got from Isabel Kerr, and therefore she was in danger and should be protected. I did not *know* he fired the shots; I don't *know* it now. As for lying, I give you my word of honor that what I have just told you is completely true. Miss Jaquette is still here, and you may see her if you have time to waste; I presume she would chaff you as she did yesterday."

Cramer looked at me. He knew from experience that when Wolfe gave his word of honor he meant it. He squinted at me, frowning, until I wondered if my tie was crooked. "I thought you did everything right," he said. "Always cocky. How much did it miss her, with you standing there, about a foot?"

What I would have liked to do you don't do to a cop, especially an inspector. All I could do was squint back at him. He got to his feet and looked down at Wolfe. "I'm still curious," he said. "You learned a lot, and of course you learned it from Cather. Do you realize that if he hadn't buttoned his lip, if he had told us what he told you, all of it, he would have been out before now, and Fleming would be in and still alive? Sure you realize it. But *you* had to do it. You had to show once more how sharp you are. I wish to God—oh, what's the use."

He turned and started for the door, but short of it he stopped and wheeled. "Don't you think you ought to send flowers to his funeral?"

I would have gone to hold his coat if he hadn't made that crack. It had missed her by a yard, not a foot. When I heard the front door close, I went to the hall for a look. He was out. I turned and called Julie, and she came around the alcove corner. There was a funny look on her face, as if she was trying to say the alphabet backward and didn't know how to start. She stopped and fastened the look on me, and I took her arm and steered her into the office. She went to the red leather chair, sank into it, and told Wolfe, "You knew that would happen. You *knew* it."

He scowled at her. "I did not. I am not a Chaldean. It was Archie, not I, who gave her the idea. 'Give an entirely different reason' was his suggestion, and she seized it. Brilliantly. Archie. What exactly did I say to X?"

"You said, quote, 'As for Mr. and Mrs. Fleming, the best I could possibly do would be to create a situation which would make it highly unlikely that they would ever disclose it.' End quote. And that he would be the judge of the situation."

"I called her a beetle," Julie said. "My God, she must be . . . first her sister, and now her husband. What are you doing, Archie?"

I had got a quarter from my pocket and tossed it up. "I'm deciding something that can't be decided any other way." I bent over for a look. "Tails. She shot him."

17

One day last week I got a letter:

> Dear Archie—
> Thanks for telling me about Orrie Cather marrying
> that airline girl. You know what I think of that but I
> wish them well, I really do. Why not? I say that to
> people sometimes, I wish you well, and you ought to
> see them stare.
>
> In a class one day last week we were supposed to
> say something about imagination and invention and I
> cleaned it up. I said nearly everything Nero said that
> day at dinner and it made their eyes pop. They don't
> know any better. I'm not sure anybody here knows
> any better about anything, but I'm giving it a whirl
> and we'll see. Somebody here must know something
> I want to know but I haven't seen any sign of it yet.
> How is Fritz? Tell him I can still taste that hedgehog
> omelet. And the sauce with the sweetbreads.
>
> Write if you want to. I wish you well.
>
> J

ABOUT THE AUTHOR

REX STOUT, the creator of Nero Wolfe, was born in Noblesville, Indiana, in 1886, the sixth of nine children of John and Lucetta Todhunter Stout, both Quakers. Shortly after his birth, the family moved to Wakarusa, Kansas. He was educated in a country school, but, by the age of nine, was recognized throughout the state as a prodigy in arithmetic. Mr. Stout briefly attended the University of Kansas, but left to enlist in the Navy, and spent the next two years as a warrant officer on board President Theodore Roosevelt's yacht. When he left the Navy in 1908, Rex Stout began to write freelance articles, worked as a sightseeing guide and as an itinerant bookkeeper. Later he devised and implemented a school banking system which was installed in four hundred cities and towns throughout the country. In 1927 Mr. Stout retired from the world of finance and, with the proceeds of his banking scheme, left for Paris to write serious fiction. He wrote three novels that received favorable reviews before turning to detective fiction. His first Nero Wolfe novel, *Fer-de-Lance*, appeared in 1934. It was followed by many others, among them, *Too Many Cooks, The Silent Speaker, If Death Ever Slept, The Doorbell Rang* and *Please Pass the Guilt,* which established Nero Wolfe as a leading character on a par with Erle Stanley Gardner's famous protagonist, Perry Mason. During World War II, Rex Stout waged a personal campaign against Nazism as chairman of the War Writers' Board, master of ceremonies of the radio program "Speaking of Liberty" and as a member of several national committees. After the war, he turned his attention to mobilizing public opinion against the wartime use of thermonuclear devices, was an active leader in the Authors' Guild and resumed writing his Nero Wolfe novels. All together, his Nero Wolfe novels have been translated into twenty-two languages and have sold more than forty-five million copies. Rex Stout died in 1975 at the age of eighty-eight. A month before his death, he published his forty-sixth Nero Wolfe novel, *A Family Affair.*